HEWEY SPADER
MYSTERY SERIES

** THE COMPLETE TRILOGY **
BOOKS 1 - 3

Tanya R. Taylor

Copyright© 2021 Tanya R. Taylor
All Rights Reserved.

No portion of this work may be reproduced, copied or transmitted in any form without the written consent of the Author.

This is a fictitious work in its entirety. The author bears no responsibility for any possible similarities concerning names, places or events.

ABOUT THE AUTHOR

Tanya R. Taylor is a Readers' Favorite Award Winning Author. She has been writing ever since she was a child and published her first book titled: *A Killing Rage* as a young adult. She is now the author of both fiction and non-fiction literature. Her books have made Amazon Kindle's Top 100 Paid Bestsellers' List in several categories and she writes in various genres including: Paranormal Romance, Fantasy, Thrillers, Science fiction, Mystery and Suspense.

Her book *Cornelius,* the first installment in a successful series, climbed to number one **in Amazon's Teen & Young-adult Multi-generational Family Fiction** category. And *INFESTATION: A Small Town Nightmare* and *CARA* are both number one **international** bestsellers.

FREE STORY!

Click the image for your FREE download.

Visit tanya-r-taylor.com to get your free short story.

EPPINGTON

THE GUARDED SECRET

(A COZY CONSPIRACY)
HEWEY SPADER COZY MYSTERY SERIES
BOOK ONE

Thank you, Rose Kenny, for all of your assistance in getting this book ready for publication and for your insight on what would work for this cover design. You are awesome and valued. xx

1

I'll never forget the day my life was changed in the blink of an eye. Before that strange thing hovered above us, we were an ordinary town with somewhat ordinary people like Mr. Mark Jeffreys who lived across the street, for example. He was a reclusive bachelor who'd obviously planned to remain one for the rest of his days. He'd already mastered the lifestyle for the greater part of his sixty-two years of existence and seemed quite contented *and conceited*, I might add. Didn't matter if he was sort of the odd one out in our neighborhood where other homes were mainly comprised of both a father and a mother, and a couple of snot-nosed kids, although there were a few single parent homes where the woman or man of the house had to courageously play both roles.

My name is Hewey, short for Hubert, but just so you know, I refuse to be called Hubert. What kind of a name is that anyway? I swore to my folks that when I turned twenty-one I was gonna change that sucky name and put Hewey on the dotted line instead. I think *Hewey* has sort of a flair to it. Don't you think? I lived with my dad and mom, Steve and Pepper Spader. They were the best parents a kid could ask for. My younger brother Carl was generally a pain in the butt, but I figured we may as well keep him since he's already here.

Anyway, I'd better tell you what happened to my hometown of Eppington a long time ago and if you ever got to know me now as an adult, you'd probably understand why I turned out the way I did. When this whole thing happened, I'd just turned sixteen and Carl was twelve. That was twenty-five years ago and I still think about what occurred back then to this very day. It really doesn't matter if you believe me or not; I just felt the urge to finally let the truth be told. Nobody else in Eppington seems to want to relive those events, but the fact that I never *stopped* reliving them probably means I'd be better off sharing with the world what actually happened. Dispel all the rumors, if you were unlucky enough to hear them. These are the facts…

2

The town of Eppington
Population: 7,572

Saturday, June 3, 1995

The four of us were the best of friends. We grew up in a community that believed in the *village raising a child concept*—which meant that Rob, Jason, Sam and I knew fully well what it was like to get the occasional whooping from random grown-ups, particularly when we were allegedly caught doing something mischievous. Subsequently telling our parents about the said whooping was a horrid mistake since that only made things a thousand times worse. Most folks back then would just compile another whooping on top of that whooping for the initial transgression. Undeniably, playing pranks on other kids and throwing eggs at the neighbors' houses whenever we felt like it pretty much fit our M.O. Mr. Jeffreys' house was mainly our target since we got the impression he thought he was better than everybody else. To be honest, we usually got blamed for everything, even when our hands were squeaky clean.

Jason, aka *Jase*, and I were the same age. He was five feet eleven; three inches taller than I was at the time. To say he was a sloppy dresser was putting it mildly. The guy didn't give one iota if his clothes were smelly or not, had gaping holes or even remotely matched. Never mind the well-known fact that his mom constantly overstocked his closet with brand new rags simply because she had the money to do so. Broad-shouldered and handsome, straggly-haired and all, Jase was unapologetically carefree and didn't have to do much to impress the girls either. I wasn't as lucky as he was when it came to girls, but I wasn't ugly either. I had short brown hair at the time, sort of spiky; a dimple in my left cheek and was more on the slim side.

Rob was fifteen, freckled face with crimson colored hair. He was the shortest in the bunch, but a nice guy whenever he wasn't hungry. Did I say, he was roughly about two hundred pounds? Nevertheless, he wore his extra poundage well, probably because as much as he ate, he was also almost equally as active. I mean... how could he not be? The four of us were hardly at home during the daytime since we never ran short of something to do outside of school.

Sam—short for Samantha—was a twin. She was sort of like the tomboy in the group. Never did anything *girlish* and literally scoffed at girls that did, including her identical twin, Taylor, who acted like a princess and couldn't keep her nose out of a book. Sam hated reading and basically only had the mindset for outdoor activities or watching action-packed movies. Just my type of gal.

Sam and I were bosom buddies from way back in grade school. She came to my defense at break time when a big kid snatched my ham sandwich right out of my hands and dashed off with it. Never knew if he was just that hungry, but I didn't care. I burst out crying right where I stood and Sam, who saw the whole thing happen, ran behind the kid, grabbed the back of his shirt and flung him onto the dusty ground. Immediately, the sandwich dropped out of his hand, so both of us lost out. The yard was still quite damp after a drizzle of rain had fallen early that morning, so when Sam scooped up a handful of dirt and tossed it into his face for good measure, I felt totally gratified. Suddenly looking deflated and now screaming like a girl, the weasel got up and ran off towards the swings where Miss Potter, a teacher, was watching her class play.

Sam hurried back over to me. By then, I'd stopped crying and she asked if I was all right.

"Uh-huh," I replied, wiping my face with both hands.

The beautiful, ebony-skinned girl actually caressed my back a bit; it was probably something she saw her folks do a lot. At that moment, I realized I was looking into the eyes of my hero and we were instant friends from that day forward. I know it's sort of strange having a girl come to a guy's rescue, but Sam was no ordinary girl. She was special.

In our town, there's a vast lake that borders a portion of our neighboring town of Crescent. The guys and I (Sam included) would usually take my Uncle Charlie's dinghy out there on the shimmering water at least once a week to fish and just to get away from all the "normal", judgmental folk for a few hours. Uncle Charlie was instrumental in teaching a lot of kids around the neighborhood who had an interest in fishing, how to do it right. He was my dad's older brother who never took much lip from anybody. Rough, thick-skinned, but had a heart of gold, he never acted up whenever the guys and I wanted to borrow his dinghy. He even owned a collection of canoes which people rented during certain holidays for spirited races across the lake.

The lake was called *Olivia*—believe it or not! It was named after a girl who'd drowned there ages before we were ever born. The talk was that her dog Ace tried to save her, but unfortunately, was unsuccessful. He did manage to pull her body out of the water though.

We were at Lake Olivia when the four of us noticed the strange, luminous, circular object hovering over our town that day in June. It was hot and sunny, but the object with its numerous miniature lights surrounding the edge of the craft glowed more brightly than anything we'd ever seen before. The steel base, as I call it, rotated slowly as it remained there for what felt like a good five minutes. Then suddenly, we witnessed a ball of light dart out of it, heading downwards like a lightning flash. The craft remained steady thereafter for another minute of two before it bolted towards the east, far into the distance.

"Bloody Mary! Did y'all see that?" Rob exclaimed.

Our jaws were dropped.

"Uh...yeah…" Jase muttered.

"What the hell was that?" Sam asked, still looking up at the sky.

"Seemed like some kind of UFO or something," I replied.

There were collective nods.

"I don't believe in UFO's," Rob commented.

"I don't either, dimwit!" Jase barked. "But does that mean we didn't see something up there that we just admitted we saw?"

"Calm down, guys," Sam interjected. "Maybe it was something sent by the government to spy on us." It sounded like she really watched too many of those action movies.

"Whatever it was, surely was huge as hell! Up close, it must be as big as a baseball field," Rob said.

I felt a bit uneasy about the strange visitor, so much so that I wanted us to call it a day on Olivia, so that I could get back home and tell my folks what we'd seen. If they'd believe me or not was another story, but I just had to tell them.

It didn't take much convincing at all as the guys all agreed it was time for us to get back. Jase lived alone with his mom. They'd moved to the area from Wisconsin after his dad went to the store for cigarettes one day and never came back. Jase seemed to have had a real chip on his shoulder because of that. I could tell it bothered him every time he mentioned anything about his dad. "Guess that store was in the Twilight Zone," he once said. "And he couldn't find his way out." That probably sounded better to him than saying his dad simply abandoned his family, leaving the two of them to manage on their own.

We rowed across the lake and with a collective effort, pulled the dinghy ashore. Uncle Charlie would collect it later that evening before dark fell, which was the usual routine. We never worried about the boat since we knew it was perfectly safe. Furthermore, Uncle Charlie lived roughly three hundred yards down the road and he could see it by walking right out of his back door.

Eppington was a place where locals were generally trustworthy and didn't do their neighbors any dirt. I did say *generally*. I heard about fifty or sixty years earlier, it was actually named 'Happy Town' by the presiding governor since it was deemed the most perfect town anyone could possibly be blessed to live in.

Crime was always on the low end and our prison compound was only occupied by about five or six inmates at a time. Prison personnel were, in my opinion, paid on slack because it was said that Brevin Forbes who'd been warden for about a hundred years had an office full of porn magazines stacked as high as the ceiling in one corner because all he did the entire day was sit in that lazy chair of his and drool over what he saw on those glossy pages.

Frank Arahna, a guard who'd put in twenty years on the job said they barely had anything to do on a regular work day because the inmates housed there for petty crimes were no bother at all. Not that the situation bugged him one bit. Wouldn't have bugged me either. Anyway, the town of Eppington was changed from Happy Town back to its original name after Governor Cleland Foulkes was elected. He wasn't as happy-go-lucky as his predecessor and in short thought Happy Town was a comical name. Guess he felt our neighbors in Crescent and elsewhere couldn't possibly take us seriously with a name like that.

"Let's go!" Jase exclaimed, leading the way as we headed through the bushes toward the edge of the asphalt road.

"You guys look worried…" Sam remarked. "What's with all the serious faces, all of a sudden?"

"Didn't you see what we just saw?" Rob asked her.

"You mean the UFO you don't believe in?" she retorted.

"Knock it off, you two!" Jase said. "Let's just focus on getting back home, okay?"

"You're worried about your mom, aren't you?" Sam asked.

Jase didn't respond.

"Look guys…I think you're all taking what we saw too seriously. Trust me, it was just one of the government's clandestine operations. Y'all can't possibly think that's a real UFO."

No one replied.

Sam shook her head. "You guys have got to be kidding."

When we arrived at the edge of the road, something immediately caught our attention. It wasn't just one thing, in particular. It was…everything.

3

Instinctively, we all halted and crouched down in the overgrown brush near the road.

"Holy cow!" Rob softly blurted. "What's going on?"

I don't know about the others, but my heart started racing. I was disbelieving my own eyes, yet *believing* them at the same time, if you know what I mean. What I'm trying to convey is that just like with the UFO, I couldn't ignore what was at least ten to fifteen yards in front of me—of *us*.

Our street was packed with animals—dogs and cats mainly, and I spotted a few squirrels and raccoons. We only saw raccoons occasionally; the li'l critters preferred their privacy even when they were surreptitiously climbing up the sugar apple tree in our backyard nabbing the delectable fruits. I didn't mind though, since I figured they also needed a belly full every few hours or so; Rob wasn't the only one.

Compared to other animals in the street, there was something noticeably different about the dogs. Although they looked like regular canines, some were on all fours as expected, but others were standing effortlessly on their hind legs. I noticed two—a rather large German Shepherd and a Labrador leaning against opposite sides of a wall and they appeared to be chatting. Yes—chatting! Not barking, but they were behaving more like humans instead of dogs. I was blown away as I watched. Our neighbors were standing in the street as well, facing the dogs who'd gathered near the eastern edge of the street, roughly six or seven feet in front of them. Other animals were sort of intermingled with the humans.

"What the hell?" Sam exclaimed. "They're all just standing there looking like zombies or something!" She was referring to the people. "And do you see those dogs? It's like they're…"

"Human?" Rob chimed in.

"Yeah."

I noticed that Jase was unusually quiet.

"There's your mom, Jase!" Rob whispered. She'd moved from somewhere in the crowd closer to the front.

"Mom…" Jase stood up and started inching out further towards the road.

I yanked him by his shirt. "What're you doing?" I whispered loudly. "Can't you see there's something wrong with them?"

"I've got to get to my Mom and find out what's going on." He looked back at me with those determined eyes of his.

"But it might not be safe," I warned.

He shook himself free of my grip. "I'm going, bro, and that's all there is to it!"

I watched worriedly as he headed toward the crowd and the rest of us moved slightly further back into the brush to avoid being seen on the heel of Jase's departure. I knew he viewed himself as his mom's protector, especially since they only had each other. So, in a way, I couldn't say I blamed him.

"Mom!" He called as he moved in closer to her.

Suddenly, everyone's head shifted in his direction, and that's when I got a better look at our neighbors' faces. There was definitely something *off* about them. As far as I could see, their eyes were eerily blank and they appeared to be in some sort of daze. A Rottweiler standing on hind legs approached Jase as he was a few feet away from his mom, who was looking at him as he called out to her, but wasn't responding. The dog was rather poised, from what I could tell, no growling or anything which might indicate he was in attack mode.

"Why isn't she answering Jase?" Rob asked us.

"Beats me," Sam replied. "They all look like they're under some sort of spell."

"Wonder where my folks are," Rob said.

I sighed. "I'd bet all our folks are somewhere in that crowd."

"You better not think of joining Jase, Rob, 'cause we don't know what the hell's going on!" Sam clearly articulated.

Sam only had to say the word and Rob would stay in line. I doubt Mr. or Mrs. Powell had that kind of power over him on a daily basis. I always thought Rob felt Sam could kick his *you know what* if she was so inclined and he simply didn't want to take the chance. Being a girl, Sam was taller and definitely stronger than Rob. I'd bet if they ever were to go at it, Sam would have him on the ground quicker than he could blink, similar to what she'd done to that boy back in grade school. Years ago, I told Rob and Jase about the incident after I introduced them to Sam and the guys instantly had the utmost respect for her.

"I'm not going anywhere." Rob had a slight crack in his voice.

I gathered he wanted to go, nonetheless, but his fear of getting on Sam's last nerve and of the bizarre situation we were witnessing just ahead, prevented him from taking the plunge like Jase did.

Jase recoiled a bit after the Rottweiler approached him. "What...is this?" He turned and asked all of them. "What's going on here?" Then he looked back at his mom, who was only staring in his direction. "Mom, what's happened? Are you okay?"

Her silence was unnerving, even for me. On a regular day, Jase's mother didn't know how to be quiet. Even though the two were close, they argued like every other Italian family I know. Jase's mother had lips that went a mile a minute and legs to match. Everything she did was as if she was running a marathon and just had to win every time. But now, there was complete, utter silence. Her lips didn't move and Jase clearly looked worried. He gently shook her as if to wake her up, but she didn't even as much as blink.

"What's wrong with you, Mom?" he demanded. He then turned around and looked at the crowd again with that Rottweiler standing nearby. "What's wrong with all of you?"

"Young man…" I heard a voice that had drifted from somewhere within Jase's vicinity. "Look at me…"

Jase turned and looked at the Rottweiler, and in that instant, I knew that's where the voice had come from. The dog was the one who had spoken!

Jase seemed compelled to look, but then I noticed that *look* turned into a gaze—one that was eerily similar to what had apparently overwhelmed the others. Suddenly, he too was silent and immediately, all eyes returned toward the area where the dogs were gathered. The Rottweiler went and reclaimed his spot before the crowd.

Jase had either willingly or unwillingly yielded to whatever control that dog had over him. He now stood there with the others, looking straight ahead through those lifeless eyes of his.

"Oh, man! Jase…" Sam muttered.

We all sighed quietly as we'd witnessed what none of us could've ever imagined would have happened to our friend. My heart was racing even more now as I assumed my folks were in that exact, same position as Jase and his mother were.

Hartley Mays, our town's police chief, was at the back of the crowd and his poodle Dolly-Ann was up front next to where the Rottweiler who'd spoken to Jase, stood.

Dolly-Ann was a rather tall poodle and certainly the prettiest I'd seen in these parts. She had a silky white coat with streaks of black, and Mrs. Mays, before she passed, always made sure her dog was properly groomed. Since she died though, Chief Mays seemed to have fallen down on the job. I personally witnessed how carelessly he treated Dolly-Ann a couple of times when I was passing his house—lashing out at her for the slightest thing. I once heard him complain that she was eating him *out of house and home*, but honestly the poor animal looked to have dropped a few pounds since Mrs. Mays had left the scene. I felt the chief was only keeping Dolly around on the count of his wife's love for her—not that he had any love himself for the poodle.

Dolly-Ann remained on all four legs as she addressed the crowd. All the while, I was looking around to see if I could spot my folks, or Sam's or Rob's, but I wasn't so lucky yet.

"In case you didn't know," Dolly-Ann started in an authoritative voice, "the town of Eppington is now under our control." A smile stretched across her face. "It's been under yours for far too long. And needless to say, but I'll say it anyway...the majority of you treated us like crap! Let's look at this as clean up time and a bit of karma, shall we?"

"Can you believe this?" Rob whispered behind me.

I shook my head.

Dolly-Ann continued, "Until our ultimate mission is accomplished—a mission you are not yet privy to—you will be subservient like we were to you and I dare say today that Eppington, as you know it, will never be the same again."

Dolly-Ann stood up on her hind legs and with her right paw, waved before the crowd and dismissed them. The guys and I watched as they immediately parted ways, all returning to their respective homes—humans and pets alike. That's when I spotted Uncle Charlie. He unknowingly walked right past us toward his house at the southern end of the street. As much as I wanted to call out to him, everything inside admonished me not to; I wasn't sure why. And within a matter of minutes, the street was empty.

"What the hell!" Sam exclaimed. "Talking dogs? And I wonder what that poodle is really trying to get at."

"We have to find out more," I stated.

Rob looked at me incredulously. "How do you suppose we do that? You saw how easy it was for Jase to fall under their spell. I'm not about to join him."

"Neither am I," Sam said.

"Me neither," I added. "But our families are out there and we have to help them any way we can."

"Of course," Sam replied. "So, what's the plan?"

The guys often turned to me and sometimes Jase for all the so-called plans. That was a lot of pressure for a teenage boy who couldn't even manage to keep his room tidy for more than an hour at a time. Mom constantly threatened to lock me out of my room and make me sleep on the front room couch. She said I needed to be more responsible and to be a better example for Carl since I was older. She certainly made being the older one seem like a chore instead of a privilege. Or is it ever a privilege? I may be confused about that, even as an adult.

"We have to get to our folks, see how they react to us and try to find out from them what's going on," I said. "Jase looked at that dog and right away, he became like the others, so I suggest we keep our heads lowered and avoid eye contact with any of the animals, no matter what. After we check out our folks, and hopefully, gather some intel, we'll meet at *the spot* around the corner in half an hour."

"Sounds good," Sam agreed.

The *spot* I referred to is an old distillery building on our block, set on a large parcel of land that's usually overgrown.

"I know you have a pet cat, Sam, but you can't interact with her until you know if she's been influenced by the other animals out there."

"Gotcha," she said.

Rob and his family didn't have pets. Never did for as long as I knew them. Rob said his dad wasn't an animal lover and was also allergic to pet fur. I always thought Mr. Powell was just a sourpuss and needed to lighten up, but I kept my thoughts to myself.

"What...what if they're able to control us without us having to make eye contact?" Rob proposed, somewhat anxiously. "How can we be sure that's what really got Jase?"

"Because we all seen it, Rob!" Sam snapped. "Why don't you stop being an airhead?"

"Look guys, we can't sit here arguing," I said. "We have to find out what's going on as quickly as we can before nightfall."

"I guess I'm ready. Well, not really, but it is what it is..." Sam announced.

"Ready, Rob?" I asked, seeing the apprehension in his face.

"I don't like how we have to split up. Can't we go together to check out our families? I'm scared."

"I know you are, but you can do this," I told him. "Just remember to keep your head lowered; don't make eye contact no matter what and if any of the animals spot you and they say anything, just act like the others."

He didn't respond.

"Remember that cool act you did in drama class a couple of years ago?"

Rob nodded.

"Man, you nailed it! You were so darn good. That's the best acting I'd ever seen, for sure! Ain't that right, Sam?"

"You know it!" she replied. "Look, Rob, you're gonna be fine. Just do what Hewey said and put on a good act. You can do this. Trust me, I'm scared as hell, but sometimes you have to do things scared. Okay?"

Rob still looked far from comfortable about the whole thing, but he nodded. "Okay."

"That's my man!" Sam patted his back.

I looked them square in the eyes. "Remember...the spot in a half hour."

They both nodded. We made a three-way bump, then hurried off in different directions each toward our home.

4

The front door of my house was habitually unlocked; we only bothered to lock it at night before bedtime. It was my job to make sure the house was secured since I was always the last one to go to sleep.

After walking inside, I noticed an unusual quietude that made me uneasy—actually more uneasy than I already was. I'd happened to get there without being noticed, as the streets were completely clear after the odd gathering just a short while earlier. I wondered where Dillinger was—our eight-year-old Doberman Pincher. Usually by now, he would've at least smelled me, even if he was out back, and would've been jumping all over me, but he was nowhere in sight.

I proceeded to the kitchen where I found Mom at the stove and Dad sitting at the counter, flipping through a magazine. He seemed to be turning the pages, but not really focusing on any particular article.

"Hey, guys," I said, casually.

No one bothered to respond.

"Is everything all right?" I waited for a few moments, then was starting to wonder if they even noticed me.

I went over to my dad and touched him on the shoulder. "Dad... are you okay?"

He flipped another page and with that blank stare I'd seen on the faces of our neighbors, he looked up at Mom and said, "Remember to make enough for four."

"Dad? You didn't answer me," I said.

"Honey, how would you like your dog food?" Mom asked me.

"What? Mom… what're you talking about? We don't eat dog food!" I sat on the stool next to Dad.

She opened an overhead cabinet and took down a couple of cans of Dillinger's food. He always preferred the soft food instead of the hard bites.

"You have a choice between chicken and beef flavoring," Mom said, either ignoring or failing to register my remark.

"I said, we don't eat dog food, Mom!" I repeated.

She politely opened the chicken flavored one. "Chicken, it is!" she said.

"Dad!" I scowled. "What's wrong with y'all? Are you gonna let Mom feed us dog food for dinner?"

Weirdly, both a happy and confused smile formed on his face. "Chicken it is," he also announced.

I quickly got up, stormed around the counter and gently gripped my mom by the shoulders. "Mom, wake up! Wake up!" I yelled as quietly as I could. "What's happened to everybody? This is ludicrous!"

She just stood there looking at me, clearly unmoved by my protest.

"What happened out there?" I insisted. "What did they do to you?"

"I have to put Dillinger's pork roast in the oven," she said with that blank stare.

"Dillinger?" I frowned. "He's eating pork roast while we're eating dog food? Have you both lost your minds?" I turned away in disbelief. "Where's Carl?"

"Out back playing with Dillinger," Mom replied with a slight smile. "I'm sure they're having lots of fun."

Seriously concerned for Carl, I left the kitchen and went to find him.

When I opened the back door, the view that greeted me was shocking. Our Dillinger was comfortably seated in Mom's white patio chair throwing the old tennis ball while Carl ran and fetched it, and brought it back (thankfully with his hand and not his mouth). Right then, to my dismay, I knew Dillinger had been affected the same as the other dogs were.

I can't believe this is happening! I thought, cautious not to make eye contact with Dillinger. By way of my peripheral vision, I noticed he was looking my way and hoped he wasn't with curiosity.

With my head lowered I said, "Carl, Mom wants to show you what we're having for dinner."

He'd just fetched the ball again and was taking it back to Dillinger. I could only imagine how many times he'd already done that. After handing the ball to Dillinger, he walked over to where I stood and without acknowledging me, headed inside the house.

I was right behind him.

"My dear boy..." I heard Dillinger say.

I knew he was addressing me and slowly facing his direction, but failing to look at him, I answered, "Yes."

"Please tell the good lady, your mother, that I'd very much prefer that special sauce she used to make for you all with my pork roast today," he added.

You would've thought he had descended from royalty.

"Okay," I said, then entered the house.

Rushing toward Carl, who'd left the kitchen and was heading down the hallway, I cried, "Carl, wait! I have to talk to you."

"I chose the beef flavored food," he stopped and said. "I told Mom."

"Forget the food, Carl. I need to know what happened to you guys. Did it have something to do with that thing I saw in the sky a while ago?"

"I have to use the bathroom, then I'm going back outside with Dillinger." There was an inscrutable look on his face.

"Listen to me, Carl. Tell me what happened," I pressed. "Do you remember?"

He scowled. "Remember? I have to remember to run Dillinger's bath. I have to remember to give him my bed tonight. I have to sleep in the doghouse."

"No, Carl. You won't! You are not the dog—Dillinger is. You don't eat dog food—Dillinger does. Wake up! They've got you, Dad and Mom messed up!"

"Dillinger's waiting. We're playing fetch," he said before walking into the bathroom and shutting the door behind him.

Exasperated, I held my head for a few seconds. "This is super crazy," I muttered. "I've gotta put a stop to this somehow."

I looked around the house to see if there was anything that appeared out of place, and was about to leave when I heard a phone ring. Moments later, Dillinger laughed.

"Oh, yes indeedy!" he blithely said. "They are all doing well. Before you know it, our kind will have everything we deserve and they will finally have everything that's coming to them." He paused briefly, then continued: "Yes, perfect location! Let them try to find it on a map."

I wondered what he meant by that last statement.

Dillinger surely surprised me. He'd been a part of our family only a couple of weeks shy of his entire life. We'd adopted him from my dad's friend Joel when he was just two weeks old and all we ever did was love and take care of him. But now, based on what I gathered from that conversation, it was clear that Dillinger was purely self-centered and to him, we were nothing special. How could an animal that was loved so dearly turn against the people that meant him no harm whatsoever? I didn't understand it—any of it. All I knew for sure was that there was no convincing my family that they were under an otherworldly spell and everything as we knew it had been turned upside down.

I'd found nothing that could possibly be of help to me and the guys in our quest of getting to the bottom of what's happened. I desperately wished that Sam and Rob had made better progress than I had. But more importantly, I hoped they hadn't inadvertently blown the whistle on themselves and had ultimately become seemingly soulless victims like the others.

5

The old wine distillery used to be in full operation for about thirty years before I was born. It actually was the property of a famous local writer who'd died and left all of his wealth to charity since he had no heirs. The three-storey dilapidated building cried out for some tending loving care which over time, it never duly received. Numerous cracked windows, aging white paint and faded wooden doors had become its modern character. The place had been sitting vacant and seemingly unclaimed for as long as I could remember.

This was our special spot. The guys and I often met there after school and on weekends. Upstairs on the third floor, was used mostly for spying on our duplicitous neighbors who snuck around getting into adult mischief whenever the "cat was away", as the saying goes. Mrs. Johnette Christie gave us lots to talk and laugh about, as well as lover boy Willie Reid—another neighbor that lived around the block with his so-called partner, but regularly found his way over to Mrs. Christie's house at 3:20 p.m. on Mondays, Tuesdays and Thursdays. With Mr. Christie being away on business for weeks at a time, their arrangement appeared to work out perfectly.

Another neighbor that kept me and the guys entertained was Julio Perez who had a long-standing beef going on with his next door neighbors, Mr. Clyde Rivera and his wife, Suzanne. Julio was a cantankerous old timer who had a problem with Christians living next to him. The guy seemed to do everything in his power to get the Riveras to sin. We once caught him peeing on the couple's front door while they were away. Another time, he tossed the biggest, dead rat I'd ever seen over the fence and made sure it landed on their walkway leading up to the porch. The guy was a real terror. One day, he took his own sweet time after the couple had left that afternoon and spray painted profanity right on their front door. We waited upstairs long enough for the Riveras to return, and saw how horrified Mrs. Rivera, in particular, was. She'd certainly had enough—enough to make her march over to Julio's front door and spew out some heavy-duty cuss words at him. I suppose he was in his living room laughing at them because he'd made at least one of them lose it.

Mr. Rivera was obviously unsuccessful in stopping his wife from going over there to Julio's place and losing her religion if only for a good, memorable minute. The guys and I wondered why they didn't just call the cops on that old jerk, but maybe they thought it wasn't the Christian thing to do. To each his own.

All the way to the distillery, I wondered if any eyes were on me, piercing my back and waiting for just the right moment to surprise me. I was nervous as heck after experiencing what I did at the house. I saw Pearl Rose's mutt sitting on her front porch staring me down, which made me wonder if he knew I wasn't the real deal. I definitely made no eye contact with him, but that wonderful peripheral vision of mine didn't leave me in the dark. That dog had it in for me; I was sure about it. Why he didn't blow the whistle puzzled me. That's why I was paranoid the entire time I was en route to our spot.

I pushed open the back door, which was our mode of entry. The first floor of the building was empty other than for scattered trash the guys and I had mostly been responsible for leaving around. The second level was full of old wooden barrels and crates, probably left behind from those days when the business was in operation. A spiral staircase was situated in the middle of the lower floor which had a few rails missing on both sides as you made your way up to the second and third floors. Sam was already there on the top level waiting on the bench we'd hauled up there the previous year and had parked right in front of the wide window facing the southern side of our neighborhood. That window offered the best view in the house and gave us a good cover too. Sitting there for a couple of hours every day offered us more entertainment than you can probably imagine.

She got up and hugged me tightly. You would've thought we hadn't seen each other in years.

"Everything went okay?" I asked.

She shook her head and I noticed she'd been crying. That was a rarity for Sam. She'd seen me teary-eyed more times than I'd ever seen her, so I knew she must've really been worked up.

"They're not acting right at all," she said, "—not even Taylor."

"I know. Same with my peeps. So, you weren't able to find out anything?"

She shook her head again. "I got nowhere. For the most part, they went about their business acting as if I wasn't even there. I just can't wrap my head around this!"

"Me neither."

"I thought I'd try and reach my Aunt Regina who lives out of town to let her know what 's going on around here, but I couldn't get a signal on my cell. So, I tried the landline in my room, but even though I got a dial tone, that's pretty much all I got. I wasn't able to dial out."

"My cell doesn't have a signal either," I said. "I don't have any contact for any of my relatives outside of Eppington and my Uncle Charlie...well... you can see he's no use even to himself right now." I paused for a moment, then said: "I heard Dillinger on the phone when I was there. I'm not sure if he was using the cordless or one of my folks' cell phones, so I have no idea if our landline is working or not."

"Your dog Dillinger was using the phone?" She grimaced. "Are you kidding me?"

"Nope. Well, we've heard the dogs talk out there in the street, so I'm not too surprised that they can use the phone."

"But who would they call? This is crazy!"

"I'd think they'd call each other. They're acting just like humans. Weird." I sighed deeply. "So, where's Rob? It's been more than half an hour..."

"I know. Sure hope he's all right," she said. "I'm really scared for him now."

I went and sat down.

"Do you think he's coming?" she pressed.

"Rob's terrified, I know, but he's a smart kid and pretty slick too. I'm willing to bet he'll be here any minute."

She shifted in her seat. "The way he was before we split, I just don't know..."

I turned and faced her. "It was you who gave him the confidence he needed today to venture off on his own, you know. He wasn't listening to me."

"You think so?" she studied me.

"Yep. Sometimes, you can really say the right words, and what you said to him made all the difference."

"Do you really believe that? I mean... that I sometimes say the right things to people?"

"'Course you do! You give me good advice all the time. How can you not know that?"

She lowered her head a bit. "I wish I could say I did the same for Taylor. Only today, I realized I hardly ever even noticed her; was always so wrapped up in myself and what interested me. She's my sister and I couldn't care less what she was interested in. And my folks... well, that's another story."

I gently placed my hand on hers. "Don't be so hard on yourself. I'm sure Taylor and your folks know you love them."

"I sure hope they do. I actually told them that before I left and they had no reaction at all—even though that's probably the first time they ever heard me say it. They barely even looked at me. I felt horrible!"

She became emotional and I tried my best to console her.

"They're gonna be all right," I said. "Somehow, we're gonna be able to fix things. I just know it."

"You're just saying that, Hewey. Even though you're an optimist, I know you. You don't have a clue about what's really going on or how to fix any of this." She was clearly frustrated.

"You're right, but I sure as heck will try and that counts for something."

She caressed my hand. "Of course, it does."

We waited for Rob for at least another twenty minutes before Sam and I became worried.

"Do you think he's gonna show?" she asked. "Maybe they got him. It's been about an hour since we parted ways."

I wasn't sure what to think, but the possibility that he'd been *influenced*, I guess you could call it, had crossed my mind from when I first met up with Sam and realized Rob was nowhere in sight. "I don't know," I replied.

Suddenly, there was a loud screech downstairs. Sounded like the door. "Someone's here," I said.

Sam stood up; a worried look blanketed her face as she stared toward the doorway.

I went over to get a peep downstairs, when I saw Rob hurriedly making his way up. "He's here!" I told her.

"What a relief!" Sam replied.

Moments later, Rob entered the room. He was sweating and looked frantic.

"We thought you weren't coming!" Sam exclaimed, very happy to see him.

"I wasn't sure I'd make it." He flopped onto the bench by the window, then focused on me. "I did everything you said; didn't make any eye contact. But I had to pass a few dogs getting to my house and then on my way here they all seemed to be giving me this suspicious look. Man! My nerves were on me. I thought they were onto me. So, I went and took the back route to dodge anybody who might want a piece of me, but then I saw about twenty dogs standing around the park and I turned back. That's what took me so long to get here."

"What about your folks? Are they under the spell?" I asked.

He quickly nodded, yet with noticeable disappointment. "They're not there, man. Believe me when I tell y'all." He glanced at

Sam. "What I saw a while ago was a shell of them. It's like something took over their body."

Sam patted Rob's shoulder. "I know what you mean. Same thing with mine. I was talking to them and it was like I wasn't even there."

"Same here," I said.

"So, what are we supposed to do now?" Sam asked.

"We have to put our heads together this time, guys. We have to do something to make our folks normal again and at the same time keep ourselves safe. The answer's out there; we just have to find it."

Sam nodded.

"Does your cell have a signal?" I asked Rob.

He slid it out of his pocket. "No, but we always have a signal in here!"

"It's not having a signal *in here* that's the problem," Sam said. "We're not getting a signal anywhere."

"Maybe the thing we saw—that UFO knocked out the signal," I surmised.

"But you said Dillinger was on the phone," Sam returned. "If by chance he was using a cell phone, it makes sense to believe that only *they* have access to the signal and not us."

Rob was flabbergasted. "Dillinger was using the phone?"

"Uh-huh?" Sam replied.

"Seems like the mutts are definitely trying to take over our town," Rob opined. "Doesn't look like cats and other animals have been drinking the same *weird juice* as they were."

"I noticed that," Sam commented. "It's just the dogs from what I could tell. Our cat, Lucy, seems like her old self. She was the only *normal* one in the house!"

"Why dogs though?" I wondered. "Why not all the animals? Seems even stranger that it's just the dogs, don't you think?"

"I'd say so," Sam replied. "Chief Mays' poodle seems to be the leader, if not one of them. The crazy stuff she said out there in the road boggles my mind and honestly scares the hell out of me."

I sat down next to Rob while Sam stood near the window, peeping out occasionally.

"I say we stay here together until we can figure out what's going on," Sam suggested.

"We'll need food," Rob submitted. "We can't stay here without food."

"I agree—which means we'll have to go back to one of our houses at least, to get the food," I said.

"We can go to my house," Rob replied. "Mom always keeps the cupboards and fridge stocked up. We can get plenty of stuff for a few days. I don't think they'll be eating it anyway."

"Why do you say that?" Sam asked.

"I think I know why," I interjected. "Some talk of dog food?" I looked at Rob.

He nodded. "How do you know?"

"My mom offered me dog food. I still can't believe it."

Sam frowned. "Are you guys for real?"

"Yep," I said. "It's all weird, to say the least."

"That's beyond weird!" Sam exclaimed. "I don't know what I would've done if any of my peeps offered me cat food! I'd tell them to get their heads checked."

"I don't think that would help, considering the circumstances," I told her. "What's going on in this town is beyond any shrink's expertise."

"What's funny though..." Rob added, "...is that we don't even have a bloody pet! And they still mentioned how we're having dog food for dinner. Guess they plan to go out and shop for some."

"That's true!" Sam's eyes widened. "Y'all don't even have a pet!"

We decided to make a move for the food after nightfall. That way, we figured we could maneuver about better without being easily noticed. After another hour or so of brainstorming and exploring different scenarios that might explain what could be happening in Eppington, there was one thing that was blatantly clear: We were only three regular kids in a town overrun by some sort of strange phenomenon. And if we couldn't get to the bottom of things soon, there was a high chance that our town would be doomed forever—and eventually, the three of us might become victims ourselves.

6

As we walked down the street toward Rob's house, I must admit, the whole time it was nerve-wracking! The guys had no idea, but every simple sound made me edgy, and at one point, my stomach felt queasy. It wasn't unusual to hear crickets that time of night, but even their chirping was almost enough to send me into panic mode. I believe what made this event more harrowing for me was that we were traveling together as a group which, in my mind, could look suspicious if we happened to be seen. There was no way we could outrun some of those dogs, especially the Rottweilers and Pit Bulls. The very thought of them catching up to us and shredding us to pieces was enough to make me find the Powells' guest bathroom the minute we stepped inside the house.

"Are you okay in there?" Sam spoke quietly outside the door five minutes after I'd gone in.

"Yeah. Coming out now." I was washing my hands.

Rob's house was one of the finer ones in our neighborhood. His dad was an accountant and his mom our high school principal. If you asked me, both of his folks seemed pretty grumpy, but they loved their Rob to bits. Gave him everything he wanted and discouraged him from being too free-handed, especially with us guys. Guess they weren't big believers in sharing, yet despite their greatest efforts, Rob was just different. He was the kindest kid I knew; would give you the shirt off his back if you needed it. All of us were pretty free-handed, I guess you could say. Probably why we remained friends for so long. We had a special camaraderie; everyone looked out for each other. It was like an unspoken pledge from day one.

Sam's nose wrinkled at the prevailing stench after I'd walked out of the bathroom. No one told her to stand guard at the door, but I guess she took her chances there rather than being anywhere near Rob's folks who were sitting together on the living room couch watching television. The only problem with that was the television wasn't on and they seemed not to notice.

Rob was busy grabbing whatever he could from the kitchen cupboards and the fridge while Sam and I waited near the front door. When he emerged a few minutes later, he was carrying two large backpacks—one on each shoulder.

"Did you get water?" I asked him.

"Yeah. I've got some bottles in here." He shrugged his shoulder to indicate which backpack the water was in.

"Let me help." I relieved him of one of the backpacks.

We headed back outside.

"Don't you think we should take our bikes?" Rob asked as we stepped down from the porch.

"And do what?" Sam glared. "Get noticed even quicker? Have you seen any other kids riding their bikes today? I sure haven't."

"I guess you're right," Rob returned. "Just thought they'd come in handy if we ever needed a quick getaway, that's all."

"We have to blend in as much as possible guys," I reminded them. "One *off* move could be the end of us as we know ourselves, then we definitely won't be of any help to our families."

As we were leaving the Powells' property and heading onto the road lined with dimly lit streetlamps and willow oak trees, an air of sadness overwhelmed me. I felt like I was abandoning my family—Carl included. I wondered what they were doing and if Dillinger was constantly taking advantage of them. A tear slid down my cheek and I quickly wiped it before any of the guys noticed. I assumed they had similar thoughts concerning their folks. None of us, including Jase had the perfect family, but we all had a family that loved us and vice-versa. I honestly didn't realize how good I had it and how lucky I was until my mother's smile was no longer there and my dad's interest was no longer in me, and Carl wasn't his annoying little self anymore. I struggled to keep myself from thinking what it would be like if they never woke up from that unearthly daze.

"We shouldn't go back the same way we came," Sam remarked after we'd already walked a good distance in the very same direction we came from.

"Why are you saying that now?" I asked her.

She didn't respond right away. "I don't know… I just feel like something's off."

"In what way, Sam?" Rob probed as he adjusted the backpack on his left shoulder.

She sighed. "Uh...forget it. I think it's just my paranoia."

We continued on.

"Hey! Somebody's coming!" Sam whispered loudly. "They're straight ahead; walking on the same side as us!"

"Just stay calm," I told them. "Keep your cool. They're probably just out for a walk."

We walked in silence and as the figure gradually approached, I heard Rob say, "It's Jase, y'all. It's Jase!"

I saw that he was right. "Still keep your cool, guys. We don't know if he's himself or not."

"Exactly," Sam agreed.

Wearing his famous grey jacket with the hoodie, Jase was walking alone with both hands shoved inside his pockets.

Before we passed each other, I stopped and said, "Jase, it's me—Hewey. Are you okay?"

He stopped and looked at me, then at Sam and Rob. They say the eyes are the window to the soul, but the emptiness I saw in Jase's probably meant that he was suddenly a human without a soul. I hated to think it, but our Jase was not present. If he was, I knew we wouldn't be able to reach him, just like we couldn't reach our folks. Without the slightest acknowledgment, he continued on his way, murmuring something about *the ninth star* or some nonsense I couldn't comprehend.

We watched for a few moments as he proceeded down the street as if he'd never known us.

"Poor Jase," Rob said. "If only he'd stayed with us…"

Sam sighed deeply. "He's too darn hard-headed! Always has been."

"Let's keep going," I said. "It's obvious talking to anyone under that spell from now on doesn't make sense. We're not gonna get anywhere with them. Let's just get back to the spot and we can brainstorm some more before the night is out."

We all got there in one piece.

The cool thing about our usual hideout was that it was never disturbed by anyone other than the guys and me. Rob had brought along a couple of search lights and even a blanket for Sam, and two sheets for him and me. We already had a few exercise mats (*resting mats,* as far as we were concerned) for when we got tired and needed a little shut eye before we called it a day and headed home. Those mats were leaning against a corner of the wall and braced by an old, white bucket partially filled with sand that had been there literally for years; left behind by someone who'd been there before we took over the place.

We also jammed a two-by-four across the inside of the door to barricade us in if we wanted no random disturbance. The famous writer might as well had left the place to us because it was just like we owned it anyway.

After we took care of some rather unhealthy snacks, we pulled out our mats, threw the covers across them and lay down in close proximity to each other, allowing a couple of feet in between the makeshift beds. With hands behind my head, I looked up toward the dark ceiling.

"I'm beat." Sam yawned. "Are you guys tired?"

"Exhausted is more like it." Rob rolled over on his stomach.

"This whole thing is enough to make anyone exhausted," I said. "You two get some sleep and I'll keep watch for a while."

"You sure?" Sam raised her head slightly.

"Yeah," I replied. "I'm not that sleepy anyway."

"Okay. Have it your way."

I realized we didn't do any more brainstorming before sleep hit Sam and Rob like a log. It probably meant, as usual, I was supposed to do it myself. I couldn't blame them for being tired. I sure as heck was, but my curiosity to fix the baffling problem kept me alert, if only a little bit. From the floor, I could see the moon and I wondered if it had the answers I needed and if, by chance it did, if it would graciously share them with me. I was desperate and determined; hopeful and afraid. I couldn't understand my feelings partly and felt lost. As I looked over toward my friends, I knew though unspoken, they were relying on me to somehow fix everything and to get us all through this. It was a hard pill to swallow, but I had to swallow it, nonetheless. They were worth it because they were more than just my friends—they were my family and we were going to stick together, no matter what.

It felt weird not having Jase here with us. He would've been up with me devising a plan on how we could possibly get to the bottom of this major mess. But Jase needed rescuing too. After seeing his mom out there in the crowd that day, his concern for her was stronger than his desire to be safe. He would've had it no other way; that's how Jase was.

Maybe when we saw him that night, deep inside the shell of the old him, he was screaming for us to save him and we just couldn't hear. I'd like to think that instead of believing he was completely out of touch with us whom he'd known for just about his entire life.

Eventually, I drifted off to sleep. The last I'd checked that night, it was 1:25 A.M. I woke up just after three o'clock and Sam and Rob were sleeping peacefully from what I could tell. I felt good about that, considering what we'd all been through the previous day.

I eased up off the mat and strolled over to the window. Looking over our street, I wondered if Mom, Dad and Carl were sleeping well. I sure wished they were. I also wondered about Sam's family and Rob's folks. I shuddered to think the Powells were still sitting in their living room at this hour staring at the blank television screen.

So many thoughts had crowded my head all at once and I sat on the bench and just gazed down at the darkness. It was moments later when I noticed a shadow swiftly move along the northern side of the Christies' house and disappear at the back. I squinted my eyes in hopes of grasping a better look, but it was just too dark, particularly around that part of the house from my view.

Mr. Christie had been out of town for weeks and rumor had it that he wasn't coming back this time. I don't know how true that was, but people in Eppington talk—a lot. And sometimes they have no inkling of what they're even talking about. We're a close community (and the best way to describe *close* is a bunch of smiling, two-faced, nosy folk being in everybody's business). My parents mostly kept to themselves for that same reason. They never could tell from day to day who was their friend and who might've been the silent enemy because everyone was so good at pretending. Eppington is my dad's hometown. Mom moved there to be with him just before they tied the knot, but she's originally from Kansas.

Further down the street, I saw a dog walking on the left side of the road; looked like a bulldog, but I couldn't be sure. And several yards down on the right was another. I assumed they might've been surveying the area for whatever reason and that there might've been more on adjoining streets. I was about to get up to do a check downstairs before returning to my mat when I heard a faint crash that sounded to be coming from the direction of Mrs. Christie's house. I peered out toward the house for a good half a minute and didn't notice anything out of the ordinary. However, I was curious to know what that sound was at three o'clock in the morning. Maybe you think I was one of those "nosy" neighbors too, but I'd say my curiosity was purely out of concern.

I took one of the flashlights Rob had brought along and did a brief check downstairs. Everything was clear and the wood securing the back door was still in place. It was almost impossible for anyone to get through the front door since it had been nailed shut and boarded up. Before going to sleep, I went back over to the window and took one last look at the Christies' house. Everything was quiet, so I went and stretched out on the mat, switched off the searchlight and soon fell asleep.

7

The next morning, for some strange reason, Mrs. Christie was on my mind. Maybe because of the crashing sound I'd heard the night before and I told the guys about it.

"Maybe we should go check on her," Sam suggested.

"It's probably nothing though," I said.

"I wouldn't be too sure about that," Rob commented as he bit into his Honey Bun—the second one for the morning.

"What do you mean?" I asked him.

"I watched this movie once where a woman heard a strange sound coming from her neighbor's house and not wanting to pry, she ignored it. Well, when the neighbor's son went to check on his mom two days later, the old lady was on the bathroom floor. She'd fallen and couldn't get up." He looked at me intently. "Suppose something like that happened to Mrs. Christie? Mr. Christie isn't here to check on her and they don't have any kids. The good, neighborly thing to do is for you to check on her; not that she's old or anything."

"She does have her lover to check on her," Sam remarked.

"Sure," Rob said. "But it's Sunday. He doesn't show up on Sundays."

"He's right," I said. "I'll go check on her."

"Want me to come along?" Sam asked.

"Sure. Wanna go now?"

"Yep." She got right up.

"I'll wait here," Rob said. "Haven't finished eating yet."

"Leave some food for later, okay?" Sam told him. "We don't wanna go back looking for food so quickly."

"There's plenty here!" he assured us, as we headed downstairs.

If Sam and I didn't know any better, we'd think it was *business as usual* in our neighborhood that morning since nothing at all looked out of the ordinary. Cars were going by; a couple of neighbors were either dumping the trash or doing something under the hood of their cars—seemed like a typical day to me. Yet there was absolutely nothing *typical* going on in our neighborhood.

"We need to venture out to see if the same thing's happening in other parts of town," I told Sam as quietly as I could.

"If we're gonna do that, we may need those bicycles after all. Besides, there's little Timmy over there on his tricycle." She pointed with her chin.

"Okay. Are you getting any signal from your cell yet? I left mine at the spot."

"Don't know. Haven't tried it for the morning."

"Try now. If you can get Rob and tell him to go for his bike, that'll save us time. After we leave here, we can meet up at the gas station around the corner and head up from there," I said.

She slid her phone out of jeans and checked for a signal. "Got it!" She smiled.

That was music to my ears.

She told Rob to head home for his bike and where we'll catch up with him. She said he sounded elated that he wouldn't have to walk everywhere we went.

"Can you get online?" I asked. "Maybe you can email one of your relatives out of town."

She checked right away, then shook her head.

"Maybe I can text though!"

Her fingers moved swiftly across the keys and I held my breath for the good news.

"It bounced," she uttered moments later with a tinge of disappointment. "If somehow I was able to get this message to my aunt, she'd be down here with major help in a jiffy."

"You tried. Something will work out."

I raised the latch for the little black gate which was approximately three feet wide—the same width as the Christies' walkway, and together we mounted the front porch.

Sam glanced around as I tapped lightly on the wooden door.

"Think she's home?" Sam asked. I could tell she was a bit nervous.

I knocked again. This time, a bit harder, but not hard enough to attract the attention of anyone that might be nearby.

We got no answer.

"Maybe she went out somewhere," Sam said.

"I doubt it since her car's right there in the driveway," I replied.

"Oh, yeah."

Deciding to try the knob, I was surprised when the door opened.

"Are we going in there?" Sam asked, reluctantly.

"Follow me."

We went inside and she eased the door shut behind us.

"Mrs. Christie…" I called out softly and waited for a few moments. Then Sam took a turn, but there was no response.

The living room was rather dark, supposedly due to the red stained cypress wood in the ceiling, which certainly added an air of elegance to the little house. I could see the wood all along the hallway.

"Mrs. Christie…" Sam called again as we cautiously made our way through the house, peeping inside of each room we came across.

It was when we checked the bedroom at the end of the hallway that we got the shock of our lives! Mrs. Christie was sprawled across the floor on her side. She was wearing a light pink and white nightgown and had large foam curlers in her hair.

"Mrs. Christie!" Sam knelt beside her.

I knelt down as well and slowly turned her onto her back. The instant I did that, we saw what appeared to be a knife wound in her chest and a trickle of blood running down the corner of her mouth. Her eyes were fixed wide open as if she'd seen a ghost.

"My God!" Sam exclaimed. "She's dead!"

I checked her neck for a pulse, then nodded. "Looks dead to me."

"We have to get out of here!" Sam cried.

Without reluctance, I wholeheartedly agreed. "Yeah. Let's go!"

We got out of the house as quickly as we could and hurried off the property onto the opposite side of the road.

My heart was racing again—even more so than when I saw the UFO.

"Do you know what this means?" Sam whispered, frantically.

"What?"

"It means that somebody killed Mrs. Christie!"

"I know that, Sam. Slow down; you're walking too fast. And try to get yourself together before you attract the wrong attention."

I know it was easier said than done because I, for one, was scared as hell. I'd never seen a real dead body before, let alone touch one. Yet, despite that, I had to keep my cool so I wouldn't be turned into a frigging weirdo like everyone else around us.

"Okay. Okay," she said, trying to compose herself.

Sam was tough. I knew she could do it.

"Hey, wait! Aren't we supposed to be going for the bikes?" she reminded me.

We were almost back to the distillery when she said it, but we had to turn back. Who can think straight anyway after seeing a dead body?

I decided it was best for us not to split up, considering the trauma we'd both just experienced. We went down the street to my house first, then planned to go around the corner to Sam's.

My brother Carl was sitting quietly on the porch with his eyes fixated across the street. Sam and I sat down next to him.

"Buddy…" I looked at him.

"Hey, Carl," she said.

He seemed indifferent.

"Are you okay?" Sam took his hand.

I wondered how he'd react to her doing that, but he was silent.

Sam looked at me and shook her head. I guess we were both hoping things would be different that day.

"Where are Mom and Dad?" I asked him, not really expecting an answer.

I got up and went inside while Sam stayed with Carl.

"Mom! Dad!" I quietly called out to them.

By that time, Mom would've been in the kitchen making breakfast and Dad would've been outside mowing the lawn. That was their usual routine on Sunday mornings. Carl would've been outside playing with Dillinger and I would've still been asleep after getting to bed around two in the morning.

I found my folks still in bed and to make sure they were alive, I stood close by and watched to see if their chests were moving. To my relief, they were just asleep.

I desperately wanted to shake them awake, but when I thought of Carl still being under that weird spell, I knew it was no different for them. My eyes landed on the telephone on their nightstand and I quickly went over and picked up the handset. I was hopeful when I heard the dial tone, but after pressing a few digits, I realized I couldn't get out. This whole thing was getting stranger by the second.

After leaving their bedroom, my mind drifted on Dillinger again.

Where is he? I wondered.

I headed out back for my bike, figuring he must be out there, and was surprised when I didn't see him. I searched the whole house and there was no sign of him. His absence, however, didn't seem to affect my family's odd behavior.

"We need to go," I told Sam, and she got up right away.

I leaned my bike against the side of the steps and went over to Carl. "If you can hear me from deep down in there," I whispered to him, "I want you to know that I'm coming back to help you, Mom and Dad snap out of this. You have my word. I love you, bro."

"See you, Carl," Sam said.

Carl seemed unmoved as he kept his gaze directly across the street, but I believed deep down he heard me and that's what motivated me.

8

Rob was waiting in the gas station yard when Sam and I pulled up on our bikes. Sam's folks were not at home when we arrived there, so we got in and out.

"What took you guys so long?" Rob grumbled.

"We have to talk," I said, "but not here."

"Where then?" he asked.

There was an alleyway adjacent to the gas station, so I felt we could get some privacy there at least for a few minutes. The operations at the gas station went on as usual, except that everybody behaved like zombies with a purpose. They knew what they wanted and got it with little verbal interaction. It made me feel for a minute there like we were in the Twilight Zone—the same place Jase thought his dad had gone for those cigarettes.

We rode over to the alley and finding the coast was clear, got off our bikes.

"Mrs. Christie's dead!" Sam beat me to the punch. "Someone murdered her!"

"What?" Rob glanced at both of us, utter disbelief shrouding his face.

"It's true," I said. "We found her on her bedroom floor." Then something hit me. "I saw a shadow of a person in her yard last night, but I couldn't make out who it was."

"Well, whoever it was must be the killer," Sam deduced.

"I imagine so."

"We have to alert the authorities," she said.

I shook my head. "If the cops are just like everyone else around here, we might be wasting our time."

"We can't just leave her dead body rotting inside that house!" Sam rebutted. "They have to get it out of there and an investigation into her murder must be launched."

"I'm for whatever you guys wanna do," Rob pledged his support.

"The nearest police station is on Meadows. We'd better head there and see what happens," I said.

Traffic back and forth on various streets of Eppington was within its normal range, from what I could tell. I couldn't help feeling that this thing concerning Mrs. Christie was going to throw us off our mission a bit, but I agreed with Sam that it would be inhumane to knowingly leave her body in the house without breathing a word to anyone.

Sam rode up front; Rob was behind her and I trailed at the back. We were riding at a decent speed and saw a couple of others out riding their bikes as well. After we entered the subdivision adjacent to ours called Kensington, which we needed to pass through on our way to Meadows, we noticed the strangest things. Dogs were up and about the neighborhood, dressed in clothing humans would normally wear. A Border Collie and what I presumed was his pup were outside on the lawn of one of the residences playing catch and he was applauding the pup for every time he caught the ball. Another dog, a Scottish Deerhound was dressed in a red blouse, and white shirt and got behind the steering wheel of a blue sedan. A canine couple were on a front porch sitting at a small outdoor table sipping a drink; and a scruffy looking one near the end of the corner was downing wine straight out of the bottle. Rob almost lost control of his bike and swerved a little. I was praying it wouldn't be the end of us because dogs were everywhere in that neighborhood. What's also alarming is that we saw absolutely no people and I wondered if they were all inside the houses or off to work while their animals took over their properties.

When we turned right onto a quieter street, I picked up a bit of speed and asked the guys if they were okay.

"Yeah," Rob replied, catching his breath. "I'd be lying if I said I wasn't nervous at what I saw back there though."

"I thought I was gonna have the runnins like you did last night, Hewey!" Sam exclaimed.

"At least we know now it's not just our neighborhood that's affected," I said. They both nodded. "Anyway, let's keep our cool, no matter what. We have to make it to the station."

Just then, the dog in the blue sedan drove past us and continued down the street.

We finally hit Meadows Ave and the police station could be seen straight ahead on the western side of the road. Rob and Sam allowed me to get ahead of them as they had no intentions of leading the conversation with the police.

We dismounted our bikes several feet away from the main door. "You two stay here," I told them. "I'll go in."

"Fine by me," Rob replied.

Sam just had a look of concern on her face. I knew she was worried about what type of interaction I might get inside the station. The cops around our parts weren't the nicest group of individuals you could find on a regular basis. Look at Chief Mays, for example. He might've been the worst out of the whole bunch!

I took a deep breath in and headed toward the entrance.

"Hewey, wait!" Sam whispered loudly. "What're you gonna say?"

"Not sure yet." I shrugged.

I knew not having a plan wasn't necessarily the wisest move in the world, but every time I didn't have one, things basically worked out for me anyway. I figured in that instance, it wasn't bound to be any different.

I walked into the station and took a quick glance around the open area. The rectangular reception desk was a good ten feet away from the entrance and surrounded by drab-looking off-white walls.

I always thought police stations had a certain air about them that I couldn't quite put my finger on. I never had any reason to step inside this one other than when I accompanied Dad to pay a visit to his friend, Joe, on several occasions. I did go on a tour to the other station in Forestville a few miles down with my seventh-grade class. Back then, I thought cops were pretty cool—that is, until I started puberty. Or maybe it was when I started getting in trouble with the guys and my mom threatened to call Joe and have me locked up for good. One time, she actually convinced Dad to have Joe stop by after work and when he showed up, he gave me a lecture I wasn't listening much to and pretty much threatened me in a polite manner.

I sauntered over to the receptionist desk where a rather lanky officer was seated. He was staring at his computer screen, then he looked up and his eyes locked on mine.

"Can I help you?" he asked monotonically.

I was shocked that he said anything. Even so, I couldn't help but notice that dead stare in his eyes.

"I'm here to report a murder...a death...at number 21 Rosemore Lane," I said. The lady's name is Mrs. Christie—Johnette Christie."

He kept looking at me.

"Maybe if you can also reach her husband to let him know what happened… He works out of town somewhere, but I have no idea where. I guess you can pull that info up on your computer somehow, huh?"

The guy seemed to be looking straight through me.

"Uh, hello…" I waved.

He started keying something into his computer. Maybe he understood what I was saying—at least, I hoped he did.

I saw cops walking back and forth mainly in the area behind his desk. All of them seemed to be in a daze and I wondered how they managed to function like that. Maybe it was an innate instinct for cops to be able to function even in such a state. My folks obviously didn't have that same instinct and neither did anyone else I'd come across lately who were under that spell.

The guy finished typing then I thought he fell asleep with his eyes wide open. He was sitting and staring at the computer screen like he was when I'd first walked in.

"Sir, did you understand what I said?" I glanced down at his computer, but knew I wouldn't have been able to see anything since the screen was facing him and not me. He seemed to just completely blank out now. What about all that kind stuff I said about cops having that innate capacity to function even in a zombielike state? Anyway, I was about to leave when I noticed something far at the back of the room.

It was a Pit Bull dressed in the type of uniform Chief Mays wore. Mays was stationed at that location, so I wondered where the heck he was—until I saw him emerge from a side door in a typical sergeant's attire. Stunned, I realized I needed to get the hell out of there. On the way, I'd thought that if, by chance, those cops were normal, I could've filled them in on what was going on and they could've somehow taken care of it. But that hope was crushed the minute I walked in.

The finely dressed Pit Bull was heading my way and I was careful to lower my head and not make eye contact even from that distance.

"I guess that's it then," I said to the guy sitting in front of me and I did a one hundred and eighty degree turn, then calmly walked out of the station.

I arched my eyebrows, hinting to the guys that we should leave like NOW. Good thing they were paying attention and we all quickly hopped on our bikes and started down the street.

"Hewey!" Sam cried behind me after we left.

"I'll tell you about it later. Let's just go!"

We were riding for a couple of minutes when I heard Rob say, "Gotta stop for something to drink. I'm thirsty!"

I slowed down, and Sam and Rob pulled up next to me.

"Stop for something to drink where?" I asked him.

The diner over there! I have money," he replied.

"Can't it wait 'til we get back to the spot?" I frowned.

"Unless you want me to fall out on this bike, I'd be better off getting that drink now."

"Let's make it quick then." I led the way across the two-lane street over to an empty parking space in front of the diner.

Fredricka's Diner was a local hotspot that was around for decades. Three generations of Forresters ran the place and kept it from looking run-down. It wasn't a large place, but was fairly cozy inside. The roof had bright red fish scale shingles and the wide fluorescent green overhang had a plastic, animated look to it. My parents actually weren't ashamed to tell me that they spent their first date at Fredricka's. Back then, they said it attracted a lot of teenagers and even had a live band several nights per week. Now, it was just a plain, old diner where waitresses ranged from the ages of nineteen to ninety. Yep—Grandma Jane was still as active as ever making sure the customers were happy. I hoped that one day when I grew up, I'd have a successful business and if I were lucky enough to have kids, they'd be interested enough to keep it going long after I passed on—just like the Forresters did theirs.

"Are y'all coming inside with me?" Rob asked.

"All of us can't go in and I'm not so sure we should," I said. "Besides, someone has to stay here with the bikes."

"I'll stay," Sam volunteered. "Not sure I wanna go in there anyway."

As always, I gave Rob a brief lecture on being cool and blending in as much as possible with everyone else. The windows of the diner were tinted, so we had no idea how many people were inside.

Eager to get that drink and knowing Rob—possibly a muffin while he's there—he opened the door and stepped inside. I followed.

What I saw almost caused me to blow my cover, hop on my bike and get as far away from that place as quickly as I could.

I nudged Rob because I sensed his struggles too, but as terrified as I knew he was, he really surprised me.

Inside the deli was a row of about ten tables and the accompanying seats located on the same side as the door. Another shorter row of tables and chairs was in the center of the room and yet another on the opposite side of the space. At the right of the door, about forty feet or so down was the large kitchen separated only by a long steel counter. And next to that was a commercial cooler filled with a variety of drinks. Dale Forrester's cashing booth was nearby. Dale was a former prom queen who graduated from our school the year before. I always had the hots for her, but she never seemed to notice. Guess Jase was more her type.

What startled me was that the tables were occupied by various breeds of dogs and the Forresters and their hired help were waiting the tables as if there was absolutely nothing out of the ordinary going on in front of them.

"I want a milkshake!" A little puppy told one of the two adult dogs at the third table from the entrance.

"Certainly, dear!" a female mutt dressed in a lovely purple sequence pants outfit heartily replied.

"Waitress!" She raised her front paw. "Please bring a chocolate milkshake for my special little guy." I actually saw a pleasant smile stretch across her well-groomed face and I nearly slapped myself in case I'd fallen asleep and all of this was just a dream.

Grandma Jane appeared a minute later with the chocolate milkshake. She said nothing and her wrinkled face seemed lifeless.

The deli was pretty noisy due to the many conversations going on at the tables and the good thing is that no one seemed to pay much attention to Rob and me even though there were no other human patrons in there. Everything inside of me screamed to forget Rob's stupid drink and get out of there at once. But yeah, like

I said, Rob surprised me. He still went over to the cooler, picked up a ginger ale and walked right up to Dale Forrester. On a low, decorative stand next to Dale's desk was about a dozen blueberry and banana muffins and what do you know? – Rob picked up three. Inwardly, I shook my head. That guy sometimes really got on my nerves. Even in a life or death situation or one that meant *sanity* or *insanity*, he couldn't seem to control himself. The whole time I stood near the door with my head lowered and only glanced up occasionally to see what Rob was doing.

When he was done and heading back my way, I started toward the door.

"Hello…" I heard someone say. Reluctantly, I looked back. My heart was in my mouth as I considered the grim possibility that we'd been found out and that might've been the end of the line for Rob and me. I thought about how close I was to the door and that there was a good chance I might not be so unlucky and could escape. But then I thought of Rob and the possibility that he might not be as fortunate since he was about a good five feet behind me. Any of those dogs could've easily gotten to him before they got to me.

"Your change..." Dale said to Rob, who I knew breathed an inner sigh of relief.

In no time, we were out of there and I don't remember us saying anything to Sam until we were way down the street.

9

"You numbskull!" I blasted Rob when we turned the bend where the distillery was.

"What did I do?" he asked as we all hopped off our bikes.

"You actually couldn't leave the muffins, could you?"

"I'm hungry. Why couldn't I get some?"

"Muffins, guys?" Sam intervened. "You're really bickering over muffins? We have more serious things to think about."

"I wish you'd get that into his thick skull!" I barked.

"They're not all for me," Rob said. "I bought one for each of us."

After that I felt bad, realizing he didn't take the risk just for himself, but for us too. I still wished he wouldn't have, but it was water under the bridge now.

"Let's just go inside, okay?" I started wheeling my bike towards the back door.

Stepping inside that diner was more terrifying for me, by far, than being at the police station. The dogs had pretty much taken over the place and although they acted like humans, I was very aware that they were still canines with extremely sharp teeth. How Rob could possibly have managed to think about his stomach in a situation like that was beyond me.

We'd come across a red and blue flyer attached to the lamppost near the distillery announcing a general meeting for the following night and that it was mandatory that everyone in our neighborhood be in attendance. The venue was one of the school campuses.

Sam had ripped the flyer off the pole and brought it inside with us.

"What do you make of this?" she asked after we sat down on the floor. "They're really taking control of this entire town, aren't they?"

"Seems so," I replied.

I took that opportunity to tell the guys about how my visit to the police station went.

"It's obvious they're taking over on a large scale," Rob said, afterwards. "If they're now in law enforcement, what else can they get their hands on that's more powerful?"

"The government," I replied. "I have a strong feeling that's what they ultimately want—to take over the government."

"From the looks of things, I'd say they've already infiltrated," Sam chimed in. "Why don't we just get on our bikes and roll on outta here?"

Rob shook his head. "We'd need a car for that—the bikes won't do."

"We can take the boat!" Sam suggested. "Before you know it, we'll be clear across the lake to Crescent."

"Too risky," I said.

"But it's right there!" Rob indicated. "I think we should take the chance. Suppose the people there are not under this crazy spell?"

I knew he had a valid point, but I also considered the possible flip side of that equation. I leaned forward. "Listen to me, guys. I feel like taking off in the dinghy should be a last resort if we can't find out more about what's going on while we're here. The reason I say that is: number one—we could easily be spotted in the lake. And what if they—the dogs—decide to come after us? There's no guarantee we'd get away. Number two: What if we actually took that chance and got away only to find out that Crescent is in the exact same situation that we're in now? What're we gonna do? Stay over there and try to find somewhere to hide out? Whereas if we stay here, at least we've got this place. And if we decide to come back since we do have this place, who's to say they won't nab us even before we get ashore? It's too risky guys. Just too risky."

"I see what you mean," Sam replied.

"Me too." Rob sighed. Moments later, he said, "But what if we managed to get over there without being spotted and the people there are normal?"

Sam cleared her throat. "That's a possibility, Rob, but Hewey painted a picture for us that it's just too risky to take the chance...and I tend to agree."

Rob looked a little disappointed. He did always have an adventurous side to him—we all did. That's part of the reason we'd been hanging out together for so long.

"Let's keep the lake as a last resort, okay, bud, considering the dinghy's still there?" I said.

"Okay." He nodded. "We could've taken one of our folks' cars if any of us knew how to drive. So, that's out of the question."

Mom had been behind me for months to take the time out of my *busy schedule* with friends to let Dad teach me how to drive. I didn't see the rush and kept putting it off for later. I surely lived to regret that one. Rob was right—taking a car might've been a breeze if one of us were able to drive it.

"Let's just focus on finding out what's really going on around here, so that if we're able to get outside help, they won't be clueless as to how to handle it," I said. "The more information we can gather, the better."

They were both in agreement.

Rob got up and sat on the bench in front of the window. "What about Mrs. Christie?" he said. "Do you think they're gonna leave her body in there?"

"Hope not." I sighed.

I'd told them how the officer didn't appear to be *completely* clueless when I first arrived at the police station, but how he was totally clueless after the first minute or so.

"Poor Mrs. Christie," Sam cried. "I wonder who did that to her."

"Probably her boyfriend," Rob said.

"You think?" I grimaced. "Why would Willie Reid want to kill her though?"

Sam got up and slowly walked over to one of the windows on the eastern side of the room. "Well, maybe he and Mrs. Christie had a falling out and she threatened to tell his partner all about their steamy love affair. That sort of drama happens all the time," she said.

"Which means she'd be exposing herself," I quickly pointed out. "She's married, remember? So, that doesn't make too much sense. Besides, do you really think anybody around here who's literally *spaced out* twenty-four-seven has the capacity to plan a murder? I highly doubt that."

"You did say the cop seemed to give you at least five seconds of attention," Sam noted. "So, it isn't too far-fetched to think someone who had it in for Mrs. Christie had the presence of mind for a short while to decide they're going to knock her off."

"Maybe the husband snuck home after hearing rumors and did the deed himself," Rob suggested.

"You mean, you think he drove on in here and acted normally and wasn't *hypnotized* by those dogs?" I proposed.

"I think you have a point," said Rob. "I don't suppose it would've been as easy as that."

The debate concerning possible suspects connected to Mrs. Christie's death continued for a while longer, then we left it alone and grabbed something to eat. The muffin Rob had bought literally melted in my mouth and went perfectly with the other junk food I'd selected from his backpack.

"So back to the subject..." Sam had a little peanut butter at the corner of her lips. I pointed it out to her.

"What subject?" Rob asked her.

"This so-called general meeting. Should we go?"

"Definitely!" I replied. "It would be interesting to see what it's all about. Maybe we'd get some of the answers we're looking for."

"I hope so," Sam said. "Don't know how long we'll be able to hide out here. No power, no light—nothing except for a couple of search lights, cockroaches and lizards crawling about at night, and God knows what else! Not the most ideal situation to be in."

You would've thought Sam wasn't used to this old place. We all were. Roaches and lizards showed up in the daytime too, so it was no big deal, at least for me.

"We gotta do what we gotta do," I said. "Would you trust going home and staying in that house with your folks right now?"

"I wouldn't!" Rob commented. "I'd have to sleep with one eye open 'cause I don't know what those people are capable of. As far as I'm concerned, they're not my folks. I don't know where my folks are."

It sounded so strange the way he said it, but I knew what he meant.

"I feel the same way." Sam stretched out on her mat. "I think I'd have to sleep with both eyes open at my house. I get an eerie feeling being around all of them."

"So, we make the best of this, huh?" I was looking her way.

"Yep. Don't have much of a choice."

We didn't venture outdoors anymore that day and with some trepidation, awaited the neighborhood meeting scheduled for the next evening.

10

Winwoood Academy's grounds was one of the most picturesque and well-manicured compared to other schools in our district. Probably because it was a private school and parents paid top dollars for their kids to go there. The meeting was set to begin at six-thirty, and the guys and I arrived there on time. We didn't want to get there early to hang around and look awkward.

Dogs of various breeds and sizes, some on all fours and others on hind legs acted as security guards and were directing everyone to gather in one main area of the campus. I felt so out of place among so many weirdos who stood there for the most part looking like statues. I saw my folks and Carl who were standing quietly ahead of Sam, Rob and me.

"Do y'all see any of my peeps?" Sam whispered.

"I don't," Rob replied, glancing around. "I don't see my folks either."

Instinctively, I looked back and toward the left, spotted them.

"They're behind us," I uttered softly. "One of the dogs is right there next to them, so don't look now."

It was an *unsettling* situation for us to be in, to put it mildly. I felt like we'd willingly, with our eyes wide open, stepped into the lion's den. Yet, we all agreed we were running out of options.

It was cool out and that was pretty much the best thing about this little gathering thus far. Inside the distillery tended to get a bit warm sometimes, even at night. I must admit though, it wasn't too bad and the mosquitoes weren't biting as hard.

I saw Sam turning her head slightly to the left, obviously hoping to sneak a glance at her family. It was sort of insane to know they were there among you, yet you couldn't be with them. And considering the way they were, I don't think any of us really wanted to. Everyone I set my eyes on out there, I knew. Miss Pinkett wore her favorite, white, old fashioned hat and a white skirt and blouse. She was in her sixties and stylish, but not in a *modern* way. She looked like she was always dressed for church, and that was sort of understandable since she was often there for one meeting or the other most days of the week. Her husband, Ted, had died in a car accident a few years earlier; they had no children. She was a strong lady though—did everything for herself at that age, even took care of the yard. I offered to mow the lawn for her once or twice, and she seemed to appreciate it.

However, I never knew for sure because she never said thanks.

Then there was tall Ralph Messi further up at the front. Rumor had it that he was about a couple inches short of seven feet. Surely looked like it to me. Ralph and his wife Cynthia, standing next to him, had ten grown children. They'd all taken off and gone to another state by the time they hit twenty. There were a lot of speculations flying around that something odd had been going on inside that house. I knew Tim and Sara well; they're the only two out of the bunch that weren't afraid to open their mouths just a little. Tim, Sara and I used to play hopscotch in the road when we were much younger. Both of them were older than me and introduced me to quite a few games, but after a while, they stopped coming out and hanging around us kids. I hardly ever saw them after that, even though they only lived a couple of doors down from my house.

The stories I relived as I looked at some of the folks around me... some were comical and others not so much.

I heard the sound of a microphone being adjusted and I looked ahead toward a podium that had been erected high enough for everyone to see those on top of it. I wasn't too surprised that it was Chief Mays' poodle Dolly-Ann that had the floor. Mays was standing behind her in plain clothing with his hands at his side. I got the feeling he was now her lackey and she must've been enjoying that immensely. I couldn't say I felt sorry for the guy since he truly was a brute. Seems like he got what he deserved, but my folks were getting what they didn't deserve because we loved and treated Dillinger well. He was a part of our family.

Dolly-Ann cleared her throat in the mic. "This meeting was called to make you aware of how things will be in this neighborhood and in this entire town moving forward. I know you all can hear and understand me, although you are limited in your response. I will have you know that this will be your new norm from now on and we, the canine species, have now been given full authority by the powers that be to control this place and to control your lives."

My heart sunk. Nothing like hearing what you kind of suspected was happening. Sam and Rob glanced my way, and I blinked quickly to remind them to keep up the act and not to show any alarm.

"Your homes are now fully ours and so are your other possessions. Many of us were enslaved by you, but the tables have now turned. You will no longer be allowed to eat at restaurants, but you are permitted to work at such places to cater to us. Social activities are out of the question unless special permission is granted by the canine officer in charge. All government appointees and officers will be replaced unless otherwise notified, but police officers will still be allowed to work and be paid, although amendments to those salaries will be made.

"Schools will carry on as usual, but will be heavily monitored and guarded by our own kind. No one will be allowed to enter or leave Eppington under any circumstances and I will have you know that this town is no longer visible on the map and no mode of transportation will be able to enter it via normal means. You need not know exactly how this has come to be; what matters is that you now have the facts.

"A survey amongst ourselves has been conducted and as of tomorrow morning, busloads of people will be transported from their homes to a facility we have ready for them. These people were selected by their dogs to be sent away for reasons pertaining to prior maltreatment and will no longer be permitted to stay in their residences. There will be no escape and no alternatives. Other neighborhoods have been notified of these implementations and are functioning smoothly as we anticipated. We are all working for the common good and to make this world a better place for dogs and other animals."

She looked at the crowd with those piercing eyes of hers: "In essence, people, you are our servants and we are your masters. You will do as you are told, when you are told."

She looked to her left at the group of dogs seated on the podium. There were seven in total. "Let me formally introduce you to our team: In the first chair to your left is our leader. He has never been adopted into any household, but has lived his entire life fending for himself and never turned his back on his two pups. He has a name, of course, but to you he is Leader and that's enough."

At that point, I felt Sam's fingers wrap around my pinky, then slowly slip away. I knew as tough as she was, she was afraid, clearly aware that none of us was any match for those guys.

The dog Dolly-Ann referred to as their leader was a Tibetan Mastiff. It had black and brown fur and could've weighed around two hundred pounds. It's long been said that Tibetan Mastiffs were the strongest dogs in the world. From the looks of that one, the saying might've been true. I surely don't remember seeing that dog or any other such breeds around our parts and I surmised that maybe he wasn't a part of the Eppington community. Their leader had a no-nonsense air about him and I definitely wouldn't have wanted him as an enemy.

Dolly-Ann went on to introduce their so-called generals, commanders and deputies. There were two Great Danes, one Boston Terrier, three German Shepherds and one Pit Bull, but none of the other dogs appeared to be as fierce as their leader. I guess Dolly-Ann was the spokesperson for the clan.

A couple of restrooms with blue signage were along the portion of the building we were standing in front of and I decided to slip away to the men's room for a minute. I assumed people still had to relieve themselves from time to time regardless of the obvious spell they were under, so I shouldn't have appeared out of place. I hinted to the guys that I'd be right back.

The restroom was less than ten feet away from where we were standing and I managed to ease away from the crowd and into the back toward the large white overhang. That particular block painted a teal color was stretched to about one hundred and fifty feet with the men's room roughly fifty feet in from the entrance gate.

I twisted the handle of the door and entered the rather spacious, and from what I could see, empty restroom. I opted for a cubicle instead of one of several urinals available. And after about a minute or so, as I was about to exit, I heard the door of the restroom swing open.

I wasn't concerned since I knew whomever it was likely wasn't a talker and just needed to relieve himself too. When I walked out, I found none other than my neighbor Mr. Mark Jeffreys in front of the basin washing his hands. I must admit, I felt kind of awkward sharing that space with him since the guys and I had gotten into a whole lot of trouble over the years for egging his house. I was glad though that he wasn't in his right mind, and that helped to ease the awkwardness a bit.

I simply walked up to a basin and proceeded to wash my hands. At that time, he'd snatched a paper towel from the wall dispenser and was drying his hands.

"Mr. Spader," he said, looking at me through the large rectangular mirror in front of us.

I was nearly frozen where I stood. The guy actually seemed like himself.

I turned and looked at him. "Aren't you..."

"No." He shook his head, knowing fully well what I was getting at. "But I was."

"So, how come you're not like that anymore?" I suddenly forgot the water was running and he gestured for me to turn it off.

"Oh, sorry," I said, turning off the faucet, then without looking at the dispenser, pulled off a hand-towel.

"I have to talk to you, but not here. It's just too dangerous. Any of them can walk in at any minute and I might not be lucky a second time."

"Okay. Where can we meet?" I asked.

"You can come to my house tomorrow morning. But then again, that might be too risky."

"Then come to where I'm staying. You know where the old distillery is, right?"

"You mean the one up the road there?" he asked.

I nodded.

"Okay."

"Can you come tonight after the meeting?"

"I don't think it would be safe. Dogs see well in the dark, but once we go about our usual business in the daytime, we'd look less suspicious," he explained.

"I see what you mean."

"Listen to me..." he spoke very softly. "I'm sure you heard them say they're planning some sort of exodus tomorrow of certain families out of this neighborhood. I'm telling you, Spader, it's just the beginning. They have a lot more in store for us."

I saw the confidence in his eyes as he spoke. "How do you know this?"

"*That* I'll explain later, but I need to tell you... you must be more careful. I was standing right behind you and your friends and noticed the slight interaction between you and the girl. If I noticed, there's a possibility that someone else might have too. Let's just hope they didn't."

I was aware of what he meant—that finger thing Sam did at one point.

"Thanks for telling me that," I said.

He nodded and started toward the door.

"Mr. Jeffreys…"

He stopped and turned.

"Come through the distillery's back door in the morning. If you tell me what time you'll be there, I'll unlock it before you arrive."

"I probably won't get there until tenish," he said, then walked out.

I waited a minute or two before leaving, and met him standing with his dog when I rejoined the guys. Jeffreys' dog was a brown Doberman Pinscher who looked like he was guarding him instead of being his companion. That, of course, was expected since humans in Eppington were suddenly at the mercy of their dogs.

The leader didn't address the crowd, but one of his deputies did. Basically, he reiterated some of what Dolly-Ann had mentioned and announced that buses would arrive at nine o'clock the following morning. By the lack of expression on those faces in the crowd, it was impossible to tell how anyone felt about what was revealed. I wasn't even sure they understood any of it, despite what Dolly-Ann had said. They almost looked soulless to me and I seriously wondered when it came to my loved ones if it was best they knew what was happening to them or not. If they knew and couldn't express themselves, I imagined the silent hell they were likely experiencing. I tried my best not to think about it.

The meeting ended approximately fifteen minutes after I returned from the restroom and the guys and I cautiously walked back to the distillery.

11

We had settled upstairs with a search light on.

"You think telling Jeffreys where we hide out was a good idea?" Rob had a look of concern on his face. "You think he can be trusted?"

"He's one of us," I replied. "Not under that crazy spell like everyone else is which means we can probably work together to fix this thing."

Sam sighed heavily. "I don't know, Hewey. Based on what I heard tonight, I'm not sure we've got what it takes to fix any of this. For one, we don't have the slightest clue what to do anyway; and two: we're out numbered."

"There must be something we can do. Maybe Jeffreys has the answer." I was hopeful.

"Doubt it." Rob sucked his teeth. "If he had the answer, don't you think he would've made a move on it already?"

"We won't know what he knows unless we hear him out. That's the least we can do," I rebutted.

I knew what was announced at the meeting pretty much knocked the wind out of Sam and Rob. I was definitely stunned at the magnitude of what we were facing too. Surely, we got some answers, but not nearly as much as we needed. We assumed that strange object in the sky had something or everything to do with it, but there was no hint as to why or how to reverse what's been done. In spite of everything, I couldn't allow myself to think that we were powerless although we were clearly the minority.

"I'd be interested in knowing how Jeffreys snapped out of it," Sam remarked. "If he did, that means everybody could, so I'm looking forward to hearing what he has to say."

"When you think about it that way, it does give you hope, doesn't it?" I said. "If everyone is able to snap out of this weird state, together we can take back our town and we won't need any outside help."

Rob's face lit up. "You two may have a point there. We may not need an escape plan after all. They're the ones that might need it."

"This all sounds well and good, but let's not get our hopes up, guys," Sam commented. "Best to just wait and see what Jeffreys says tomorrow."

I agreed. There was nothing worse than dashed hopes.

* * * *

That night, something summoned me from my sleep. I'm not sure if I heard something or sensed it, but rubbing my eyes, I got up from the mat and sauntered over to the window.

Down the street, I immediately noticed a white van was parked in front of Johnette Christie's house. And moments later, two men emerged from the home carrying a stretcher with what looked like a body on top. I assumed it was Mrs. Christie's body on the stretcher, but wondered why they'd chosen to collect it in the middle of the night. Two dogs, walking on their hind legs were with them and after one of the animals opened the back doors of the vehicle, the men lifted the stretcher inside. One of them must've hopped in the back as I only saw the two dogs and the other man appear at the side of the van. The dogs entered through the passenger doors while the man took the driver's seat. I heard the engine start and they drove away.

I quickly went over and nudged Sam. She woke up right away, a bit startled.

"They just came and got Mrs. Christie's body," I told her.

"They did?" She seemed a little surprised, considering how sleepy she obviously was.

"Yep."

"Okay, that's good then." She yawned. "Go back to sleep. We'll talk about it in the morning."

She rolled over and moments later, I heard her snoring.

It wasn't easy for me to fall asleep again. In fact, I stayed up a long time as my thoughts were all unsettling.

* * * *

The next morning…
8:58 A.M.

The roar of buses broke through the silence of our neighborhood and the guys and I rushed over to the window overlooking our street.

Five big, yellow school buses pulled up one after the other, parking on the western side of the street. I noticed the last one had stopped directly in front of my house.

None of us spoke a word as we watched and waited to see what would happen. Soon, the first bus drove off and pulled up on the opposite side of the road in front of the McIntosh residence, then the second drove up to the second house on the western side of the street. The third one moved next, stopping in front of Joe and Betty Kincaid's house and the last two remained where they were.

Nervously, I watched, hoping for that last bus to drive away, but then like clockwork, several large dogs exited each bus and walked towards the homes they were parked in front of.

"Oh, no!" Sam muttered, glancing my way.

I said nothing; only watched. Then within a couple of minutes, I saw my parents and Carl being escorted out of our house. They were walking quietly and submissively toward the bus with suitcases in hand.

"I'm sorry," Rob said, as I felt the anger building inside of me and the tears simultaneously flowing down my cheeks. I hated what was being done to them and the fact that there was nothing I could do to stop it. The guilt I harbored was overwhelming and I desperately wanted to run down there and fight as hard as I could to save my family, like any of them would've done for me if I was in that exact, same situation. I was a failure as a son and a brother.

We continued watching as all the families they came for were driven away, one bus behind the other, and we had no idea where they were taking them.

Sam placed her hand in mine. "Hewey, I'm really very sorry," she said. "I wish there was something we could do…"

I shook my head and sat on the bench. "I won't let them get away with this. Mark my word. I'm gonna find out where they're taking them and I'm bringing them back home."

Rob sat down next to me. "I'm with you, buddy. We'll find a way to fix this just like you said."

Sam nodded. "When they hurt one of us, they hurt all."

I sat alone while Sam and Rob got a quick bite to eat before Jeffreys was due to show up. I didn't have much of an appetite—at least, not for food.

Around 9:50, we heard the back door open and Rob hurriedly went over to the stair rail to see if it was who we were expecting.

"It's him!" Rob whispered.

"We're up here!" He told Jeffreys, seconds later.

Jeffreys walked in with his Doberman Pinscher and we all panicked the moment we spotted the dog. Rob had not mentioned it was with him and I wondered if he'd even seen it.

"Don't worry," Jeffreys said, noticing our apprehension. "Hugo's no threat."

Baffled, the guys and I glanced at each other.

"Do you mind if I take a seat?" Hugo asked.

Startled, although I shouldn't have been, I answered, "No. Go right ahead."

Jeffreys smiled, albeit slightly and took a seat on a chair on the side of the wall while Hugo sat on the floor nearby.

"I think you all had better sit down for this," Jeffreys said.

The three of us sat on the bench at once.

Jeffreys crossed his legs. "Spader, I can tell from the look on your face that you know they've taken your family away and I'm very sorry about that."

"Yeah." I nodded.

"I believe we know where they've taken them, but I can't be sure until later on," he returned. "But before we get into that, I think I ought to let you know what happened to me. Do you mind if I smoke?" He pulled a cigarette out of his shirt pocket without awaiting a reply, reminding me of the reason why we found it so easy to egg his house over and repeatedly. The man acted obnoxious, but right then, I couldn't care less about his flaws. I wanted to hear what he knew.

"We don't mind," I said anyway.

"Well, I'll have you know that I was no different from everyone else around here after some aircraft hovered over this town." He lit his cigarette. "Whatever it emitted apparently put all of us in a daze and, in turn, enhanced the minds of dogs to match our intellect. That's why you see people and dogs acting the way they do."

"So, it definitely was a UFO?" Sam sought clarification.

"If you can call it that." He nodded. "It came here to accomplish a strategic mission which has to do with setting things quote unquote *right* as far as canines, in particular, are concerned."

"But why?" Rob interjected.

"May I answer that?" Hugo asked Jeffreys.

"Sure, Hugo. Be my guest." Jeffreys gestured with an outstretched arm.

"The reason for all of this has to do with the handling of dogs in this town over the course of time, where we were grossly mistreated, unappreciated and taken advantage of," Hugo started. "The opportunity, long-awaited, finally came for us to settle the score by placing humans in a subservient state and for the first time, allowing dogs to rule. Does that explain your question in a nutshell?" he asked Rob.

Rob quickly nodded.

"But how is the UFO connected to all dogs here in Eppington and how did you escape from their hypnotic grip, Mr. Jeffreys?" I asked.

Jeffreys looked at Hugo and smiled. "It's because of Hugo here," he revealed. "He saved me."

"I couldn't bear to see him the way that he was," Hugo chimed in. "To me, he wasn't my master or my friend anymore and having control over him that I never asked for didn't sit well with me. I wanted the old him back and I opted to take the risk."

I was amazed at how well he spoke—actually, by how well they all spoke, even Dillinger.

"So, I did what I knew I could to relieve him of the so-called spell," Hugo continued.

"And how did you do that?" Sam asked, eagerly.

"I'm not quite sure, to be honest. I just know I started to reflect on all the good times we had since he first brought me into his home and how much I loved him and he loved me. Instinctively, I inwardly relinquished my powers and professed that Mark here was my master. That's simply what I did—all it took."

"Yes, he told me the same thing," Jeffreys affirmed. "All I knew was that I was back to myself, but Hugo and I both had to continue the act if we were going to be safe."

"Interesting…" Sam said.

"So, that means the power to release everyone is in the hands of their pet dogs?" I asked.

"You're absolutely right!" Hugo responded.

"What about people who don't have dogs?" Sam noted.

"The leader has the power to relinquish that hold on them," Hugo answered.

Sam shook her head disappointingly "I guess getting my peeps released is hopeless since the leader's not about to do them any favors, huh?"

There was a brief lull in the conversation, then Jeffreys said, "I wouldn't be too sure about that just yet."

I thought of our dog, Dillinger, and how he had the power to release my family and didn't. I couldn't fathom what on earth had made him turn on us like that and I felt betrayed. How he could do this befuddled me.

"Do you remember how it was when you were dazed?" I asked Jeffreys; my curiosity piqued.

"I do." He nodded. "I heard things, but it took a while before they registered and most times, I don't think they ever did. Although I knew something was terribly wrong and felt helpless, I was unable to express myself in any way. There was a numbness inside—an emptiness I can't quite explain and I just couldn't break out of it no matter how hard I tried."

I lowered my head momentarily, as I imagined my parents, Carl and Rob's and Sam's family experiencing the same thing.

"You're in a shell and sort of pushed down near the bottom," Jeffreys continued. "Guess that's the best way to explain it."

I looked at both Jeffreys and Hugo. "They've got my family and I'm gonna do whatever it takes to rescue them. When will you know where they are?"

Jeffreys uncrossed his legs and leaned forward in his chair. "Hugo gets intel about all the latest developments; one of the generals keeps him informed. As soon as we find out where they are, I'll let you know, but you can't just go barging in there. You need to have a plan."

"I hear you."

"Is there any way we can just grab our folks and get out of this town?" Rob asked.

"You'd be able to drive us right out of here, won't you?"

"There's no driving out of here nor getting in, Powell," Jeffreys replied. "Do explain, Hugo."

Hugo rapidly blinked his eyelids a few times, then answered, "Mark's right. An invisible barrier now exists between this town and the rest of the world. Cars are unable to find a road that leads into this town and vice-versa. Even planes, once they take off, will fly into nowhere and disappear. This town of Eppington has been hidden behind the barrier."

"Holy cow!" Rob exclaimed before looking at Sam and me. "That means if we'd rowed across the lake to Crescent, we wouldn't have gotten in…"

"Exactly," Jeffreys replied. "It's a really disturbing situation."

Everyone was quiet and obviously in deep contemplation.

"Hugo and I have discussed this in great detail and we believe there may be a way to get us all out of this hot mess." Jeffreys finally broke the silence. "For just the two of us, it would've been quite a hefty challenge, but with all of us, we stand a better chance."

We were all ears as he explained what must be done.

KEEP READING FOR BOOK TWO IN THIS EXCITING SERIES!

EVERY DOG
HAS ITS DAY

HEWEY SPADER COZY MYSTERY SERIES

BOOK TWO

1

Jeffreys and Hugo had given us much food for thought. I could hardly believe my ears as I listened to them, but it was comforting to know that based on their experience, there was hope left for the rest of us.

It was abundantly clear to me that my dog, Dillinger, would have nothing to do with helping my folks, so relying on him for anything was completely out of the question. I imagined he was relishing the idea of having our house completely to himself. I couldn't help thinking he'd better enjoy whatever time he had left, because I was going to find my folks, get to the bottom of this lunacy and we were going to reclaim our home and this town. Afterwards, if I had anything to do with it, Dillinger was going to be shipped out. Yeah, every dog has its day.

It had been three days since we'd heard a peep from Jeffreys and I was starting to wonder if Hugo had yet been informed as to where they'd taken my family. The guys and I had moved around very little since the neighborhood meeting and I was beginning to get more agitated.

"Who are you calling?" Sam asked after I picked up my cell from the bench near the distillery's upstairs window.

"I need to find out if they know anything yet," I said.

Standing with her arms folded and a reprimanding look on her face, Sam replied, "Hewey, put the phone down. Jeffries specifically told us not to call. He said he'd be in touch. Don't you think he said that for a reason?"

I sighed heavily. "Why hasn't he gotten back to us?"

"Maybe because they haven't found out the location yet."

Rob emerged from the bathroom with a large white towel wrapped around his waist. It was amazing that the well water still ran through the pipes of that abandoned building. Although it was sort of hard and the smell wasn't the best, it was good enough for us to stay somewhat clean while we crashed there.

"What's going on?" He was drying his hair with a smaller towel. Good thing he thought to bring some soap and shampoo along that night when he'd grabbed the food.

Sam came over and sat next to me. "Hewey's tired of waiting for Jeffreys to get back to him," she explained.

"It's been three days! I was wondering what the holdup was myself." Rob reached for some clean clothes he had laid out on his mat.

"There's no use getting impatient, guys." Sam glanced at us both. "I'm eager as hell to know where Hewey's peeps are too, but we can't go calling the man when he specifically said not to. If we trusted him thus far to have him come over here and pretty much expose our hide out, we need to trust him some more."

"You think he's gonna come through then?" Rob seemed a bit curious.

Sam nodded. "I think so. At first, I wasn't too sure about him, but after they showed up and explained how things went, I kind of felt better about the whole deal."

I sat quietly, sliding my thumb across my cell phone's screen.

Sam looked at me. "You're having doubts about Jeffreys?" she asked.

It might've taken a good ten seconds before I responded. "I don't know. I thought by now we would've heard something from them. I keep wondering where my folks are and how they're doing. I wonder if they're being treated well or not and what their living conditions are like."

After slipping his blue tee shirt over his head, Rob sat down on the mat and crossed his legs.

"We need more food," he said.

Sam was glaring at him. "We're talking about Hewey's peeps here and you're thinking about food? Really, little boy?"

"I mean...I feel for Hewey and I'm just as worried about his folks as much as you are, but we can't help anyone if we starve to death!"

"Who's gonna starve, you dimwit!" Sam lashed out. She shook her head frustratedly. "I just can't believe you sometimes, Rob Powell. You act like your brain is in your butt and you're always sitting on it. Take your mind off of food for a while, okay? There are more important things for us to think about."

"He's right," I interjected.

"What?" Sam looked at me as if I'd said a forbidden word.

"Rob's right. We need more food."

Her eyes blinked rapidly for a few seconds. "Wait! Let me make sure I understand this. A couple of minutes ago, you were all distressed about not knowing where your peeps are; so much so, that you were about to do the one thing Jeffreys told you not to do. Now, you're thinking about food. How does that compute? Does your brain click off too like this wise guy's," she pointed, "whenever your stomach growls?"

I shook my head. "Of course, I'm totally concerned for my folks, but we're literally down to the last Honey Bun and there's no more drinking water. If we're hungry and thirsty we're not gonna think straight. We need to go and get some supplies, just like Rob said."

She looked outside the window, then glanced at her wrist watch. "It's a quarter past ten. The neighborhood doesn't look so busy. You want us to go now or wait until nightfall?"

"Jeffreys did say it was riskier moving around at night, so I guess there's no better time than the present," I said.

"Wait a minute."

She stood up. "Whose house are we going to this time?"

"We can't go to mine. I don't know how things will go if we do with just Dillinger there now."

"We can go to my house," Sam suggested. "Guess, we'll have to rotate between Rob's and mine."

Rob grabbed his backpack and got up. Sounds like a plan. Are we ready then?"

I slid my cell into my pocket and we headed out.

2

We decided to leave the bikes this time since we didn't have too far to go. If we didn't already know what was going on in our town, we would've thought everything was as normal as normal could be. Our street was quiet, for the most part, with several pedestrians walking along the sidewalks. A couple of kids were outside quietly standing around, while I imagined most of them would've been in school since it was the middle of the week. On the weird side, a few dogs seemed to be doing odds and ends around the yard, specifically at those residences where we'd seen the buses collect the human inhabitants. I figured the dogs left behind were picking up where their owners had left off. I could see my house further down the street and there was no movement on the grounds. I envisioned Dillinger inside watching an exciting movie or funny sitcom with his hind legs elevated. I hated the thought of him enjoying life to the fullest in the house my parents worked hard to build while they were somewhere they didn't deserve to be at. The whole thing was so unfair.

We passed Johnette Christie's house which was locked up since she'd unwillingly vacated the premises. Then, there was Jeffreys' place a couple of doors down on the same side. He had an average-sized, blue trimmed white dwelling with fancy iron shutters looming over the top-edge of the windows. The yard was enclosed by a four-foot high blue concrete wall. I was tempted to stop by and find out what was taking him so long to get back to me.

"Don't even think about it!" Sam quietly snarled.

She knew me all too well. Rob was walking closely behind us, but not close enough to arouse suspicion. He'd pretty much mastered the "play it cool act" which made our movements out and about seamless.

Suddenly, behind us, I heard a police siren sound then abruptly stop. At that moment, I was left with the terrifying decision to look back or to keep walking as if I hadn't heard it. Without turning my head, I glanced at Sam.

"Just keep walking guys," she said. "Don't look back. Just keep going."

I thought that was smart advice and was impressed that she took charge.

"I ain't lookin' nowhere," Rob asserted. "I don't care what!"

"That a boy!" I told him.

The vehicle was approaching and this heart of mine started its usual pounding like when I was about to piss my pants from fear. "Stay… stay cool." My voice was shaking. "Don't look at them even if they address you."

I was wondering if it was a good idea after all to listen to Jeffreys when it came to going about our business during the daytime. I still felt that sneaking out at night was a wiser decision. Too late now.

The vehicle now slowly moved alongside us. I could feel the pebbles of sweat sitting on my forehead and more at the nape of my neck, and was praying I didn't look as nervous as I was.

"Halt!" went a male's voice from the vehicle, which my peripheral vision confirmed was, in fact, a police squad car.

The three of us stopped in our tracks and as if reading each other's thoughts, none of us turned in the direction of the vehicle.

"Where are you headed?" the person asked.

"To my house," Sam answered, standing as stiffly as a robot. She almost sounded like one.

"Where is your house?"

"Down the street; left at the T-junction."

"Where are you all coming from?"

A few seconds passed and I wondered if I needed to interject, then Sam replied, "The basketball court."

I really wasn't sure that was the best answer, yet I had no idea what I would've said.

The next twenty seconds were practically the longest of my entire life. I shuddered at the thought of him getting out of that car and forcing us into the back seat. Carl and my folks flashed through my mind. The thought of my being prevented from helping them was devastating—not so much being stripped of my own freedom.

"Very well. Carry on then," he said.

I breathed a huge sigh of relief.

As he drove off, I caught a glimpse of a large canine in police uniform. From what I could tell, there was no one else in the car.

"I nearly pissed my dang pants!" Rob exclaimed as we continued walking.

"That makes two of us," I said.

"No—three," Sam added, then she looked my way. "I wonder why he let us go."

"Because we put on a great act, obviously!" Rob told her, smiling.

By now, the squad car had turned the bend at the end of the street.

"Okay, big guy. Calm down," I said. "You wouldn't wanna have survived that only to blow our cover now. You never know who's watching."

"Okay. You're right," he agreed.

"Do you think we were really that good?" Sam asked me.

"I guess so. Besides, we've had almost a week of practice. I gave her a long glance. "What are you thinking? Why else would he just drive off? I'm pretty sure if he suspected there was anything suspicious about us, he would've taken us in."

"I don't know. Just had a funny feeling about it. I'm still a bit shaken up by the whole deal."

"He's gone, so we're safe," I said. "Let's just get to your house and hurry back."

I'd missed being able to stroll through our neighborhood without fear of being noticed. Seemed like gone were the days when we went outside into the hot sun and busied ourselves doing mischievous things we later got punished for. I missed all the reprimanding from my mom, in particular, and from a few of the grumpy neighbors who seemed to get *off* on me being told a thing or two or getting a good whooping for allegedly doing wrong things. I missed my dad's laid-back behavior about the whole thing until Mom got on him, telling him how he'd spoiled me and would later on regret it. I missed all that. I especially missed Mom's home-cooked meals. My favorite was lasagna and curried steaks. I even missed Carl; he was an okay li'l brother.

I snapped out of my seemingly endless reveries when we got to Sam's house. Looking on from the edge of the street, I had an eerie feeling inside. Although most of the homes these days were quiet, Sam's house was *unusually* quiet. I wondered if the guys had the same feeling I did. I kind of got that impression from Rob—how he stood there a few moments just as I did before proceeding onto the lawn. Sam was already almost midway to the front porch.

She glanced behind. "Are you guys coming or are you gonna stay there?" she asked.

Rob and I looked at each other. "Well, are you comin'?" he asked me.

I nodded. "Uh-huh."

Not a single person in the vicinity of Sam's house was outside, neither were there any dogs. We had grown accustomed to at least seeing the canines out while the humans were off somewhere doing whatever, albeit in a dazed, somewhat robotic fashion. I wondered why that day was so different, simultaneously wondering if anything around our community would likely remain constant or the *new norms* will forever be changing. It was a worrying thought and one I shook out of my mind, at least temporarily, to focus on the task at hand.

On the porch, Sam knelt down slightly and retrieved a single key from under the light brown welcome mat. She then unlocked the door and went in. We stepped inside behind her.

"Close the door, Rob!" I said, as he was the last to enter.

"Kay, dude. Chill out," he replied, aware of my agitation.

I admit, I was a bit on edge there which was unlike me, for the most part. Mom always said I took right after Dad, being laid-back and not allowing things to get me riled up like she often did. If I didn't wash the dishes when she asked me to, I was "rude" or "disrespectful". She came from the old school where kids jumped when their parents said the word; no questions asked and no back-sassing. Mom constantly told me and Carl that as if she grew up in the perfect era and kids from her generation turned out so wonderful. Her famous words were: "You kids today have it too good!" I wonder what she would've wanted. For us to grow up a square like she was? Anyway, I was good at letting her just run on until she realized we weren't listening—at least, I wasn't—then she'd find something else to do. She was such a special lady and I never imagined in a million years that I'd get tired of her scolding me. I had to get my family back even if I died trying.

My middle grade teacher used to say, "You don't miss the water 'til the well runs dry". I'd never really grasped what that meant until I'd lost the people who loved me the most.

Sam called out to her folks as we proceeded to walk through the house. We could've heard a pin drop for how quiet in there was.

She checked all of the bedrooms, then went and opened the sliding door that led out back where their swimming pool was. The property was enclosed by a five-foot high white concrete wall, except for the front of the yard which was left wide open. We all stepped onto the back deck and looked around the large yard. Sam's dad took special pride in their surroundings. He was in the yard doing something nearly every time I showed up at their house on weekends. The lawn was a brilliant shade of green and was always properly manicured; he personally saw to that. A variety of plants stood proudly throughout the yard, none more than four feet tall and all had their own red mulch surrounding them on the ground. There were a few small window boxes of flowering geraniums, mainly in the front part of the house, but a couple along the back as well.

The pool guy was there every weekend—yes, every single Saturday without fail, as Mr. Turner had educated himself about waterborne diseases and was a stickler for having a clean pool at all times. Furthermore, Sam said that was his oasis almost every evening after work, once the weather was good.

The spa connected to the pool was reserved for use only by the Turner family. Mr. Turner made that clear from the very first time I'd stepped foot in their backyard, but I didn't mind, particularly since the pool wasn't off limits to Sam's friends. Sam, Rob, Jase and I had spent many hours in that pool and just being out there that day made me wonder if the four of us will ever share those moments again. Having Jase out of the picture felt weird, by far. Yep! That thought crossed my mind again—*you don't miss the water 'til the well runs dry*.

"Where the hell are they?" Sam cried, clearly worried.

"They probably just went out," I said.

"You mean for a walk?" She arched her eyebrows. "Both of my folks' cars are parked in the driveway and they don't go for walks unless they drive to the park and walk there. And where's Taylor? Certainly, she isn't out walking!" she exclaimed. "The girl hates walking from her bed to the bathroom when she needs to!"

I went over to Sam and rested my hand on her shoulder. "Sam, let's not let our minds wander off in the wrong direction. I know it looks strange, but considering the mental state they're all in, there *is* a possibility that they could be doing things they wouldn't normally do like going out for a walk around the neighborhood, for instance. How about we just wait here for a while until they come back?"

Rob came over. "Hewey's right, Sam. We shouldn't expect our folks to be acting the way they normally would have before all this crap happened. Nothin's normal around here anymore." He had a somber expression on his face.

Sam looked at both of us, a slight frown on her flawless face. "I hope you're right." She sighed. "You know what? I don't even see our dang cat! Maybe it went for a walk too, huh?"

She called out to their cat, but it was nowhere in sight.

We sat out back with the sliding door ajar, just staring out at the pool and reflecting on how life was for each of us before we saw that thing hovering over our town. Rob had helped himself to some bread and jam a couple of times while we waited, and with Sam's permission, he packed up some food in his bag for us to take back to the distillery. He'd even sat in the TV room for a while watching cable with the volume turned down low.

Sam's house was cozy and always tidy. They had a housekeeper, Mary Lou, who'd been with them for more than a decade and came in once a week on Thursdays. She was in her fifties; had a multitude of health issues, but could still work like a horse. Sam's folks had even paid for a surgery she got some years ago that her insurance didn't cover much of. She was obviously more than a housekeeper to them, but a friend. She even had a certain level of authority over Sam and Taylor, I suppose since she was around them from they were very young. Sam had said that even though Mary Lou was the housekeeper, she made her and Taylor know that she expected the house to be clean whenever she came over. In other words, she wasn't picking up after any nasty kids. I guess in the long run, that threat might've benefitted not just Mary Lou, but the girls too. Sam couldn't stand disorder in any sense of the word, and of course, Taylor was a little princess in her head and princesses weren't nasty.

Mary Lou didn't play around. She even got on me once for not fixing a chair on the patio that I'd moved from one spot to the other. With a stern expression on her little round face, she said: "Young man, did you meet that chair like that?" I looked at the chair and back at her. "No, ma'am," I replied. She puckered her lips and craned her neck. "Well, if you don't want to go tumbling over the front lawn, you'd better fix it back how you met it!" She didn't mince her words. Reminded me of Sam—and I truly liked that in a woman. I heard more than once that a lot of men can't deal with strong women, but I wasn't bound to be like a lot of men. I loved me a strong, bullheaded woman to keep the excitement in the relationship and to sort of keep me in line. Having a balance is good, especially since I knew I had the tendency to do some pretty stupid things at times.

"It's been a whole hour and they're not back yet!" Sam grumbled. "Where the hell could they have gone?"

Clueless at that point, I only sighed.

"How much longer are we supposed to just sit around? If, by chance, they went for a simple walk, they would've been back by now." She got up the way a fifty-year-old would. "Let's go inside. I'm tired of being out here."

I followed her inside and locked the sliding door behind us. She sauntered over to the one of the living room windows where a gold valance hung. "Don't you think it's odd that no one around here is outside?" she asked.

I joined her over at the window. Rob was still in the TV room. "I thought you hadn't noticed. Struck me as soon as I got here." Then I had an idea. "How about Rob and I sneak over to a couple of the other houses and see if anyone's inside. We can just peek through the windows? The ones that don't have dogs, that is."

"O...kay..." she gave me a curious look.

I knew what she was thinking.

"If other houses are empty, then I guess we can assume something's up, huh?" she said.

"Maybe—provided their cars are also in their yards."

I went over to Rob. "Let's go, buddy."

He seemed bothered by my presence. It was obvious that I was interrupting his program. "We're leaving now?"

"Not for good. You and I are gonna walk calmly over to a couple of the neighbors' houses and see if it looks like anyone's home. Pay attention to the driveways—if there are any vehicles in the yard. Sam's staying here 'til we get back." I revealed what we hoped to accomplish.

"And what if someone's home and sees us walk into their yards?" he asked.

"Just act dumb. Say I'm sorry, wrong house, or something and leave."

"Sounds like great advice to me." He shook his head.

"You know how to act, Rob. I don't have to spoon feed you anymore."

He got up and we headed out.

3

I decided I'd take two houses on the same side as Sam's while Rob took two across the street.

Will and Naomi Washington never owned a pet as long as I knew myself. They had four grown children, two of which were still at home living off of *Mommy and Daddy*. Manny Washington was almost thirty-five and his sister Beth was hitting forty. They looked just like they acted—*lousy*. None of them seemed to be able to keep a job, while the other two kids were off on their own acting like real adults. Word was the ones that didn't live there treated Mr. and Mrs. Washington pretty good and helped out with the upkeep of the house since their folks were at an advanced age. I saw Mr. Washington pushing a lawn mower while Manny sat in a chair outside with his dirty feet up on the outdoor table. Beth stayed in pajamas every time I saw her around the house, while Mrs. Washington took care of things, such as cooking and cleaning. How fifty percent of those kids could've turned out one way and the other fifty percent turned out completely different boggled my mind. I figured though, that the Washingtons might've spoiled Manny and Beth, considering they were the youngest. Fortunately, for my brother, Carl, he wasn't able to get away with much since our folks treated both of us pretty much the same. I couldn't imagine any of us growing up only to turn out like the Washington simpletons— Manny and Beth.

Since I was in pretty good shape at that age, I simply jumped over a couple of fences to get to the Washingtons' residence. They didn't have a fence, but I made it through the Carlsons' back yard to get there. I figured walking the front strip might've been too open, especially when moving from house to house. I'd told Rob we were to walk in the neighbors' yards, but although I mostly "jumped" into them, I knew he couldn't, so it doesn't matter. The Carlsons were taken the same day my parents were, leaving behind their German Shepherd whose attention I was careful not to attract as I entered their yard. There was a fair amount of tall bushes at the back of each property on that side of the road, which was a good cover for me.

The Washingtons' house was all white. Not as large as Sam's, but just as nice. Thanks to Mr. and Mrs. Washington and their two responsible children. From the eastern side of the house, I noticed the blue Dodge Caravan on the driveway—the elderly couple's only vehicle which Manny and Beth occasionally used as well. That residence had the same quiet, eerie feel that Sam's house had just before we entered it. I think I knew the answer to whether or not anyone was at home before I even bothered to check. The windows at the back were widely ajar and through parted vertical blinds, I was able to get a good view inside. Right away, I figured I must've been looking in at Manny's room. A guy's clothes were strewn about the place and it looked as if a category five hurricane had barreled through. No one was in sight though. So, I moved on to another side of the house and was able to peek into a different window.

That room was the complete opposite of the first one I'd seen. I figured it was either old Mr. and Mrs. Washington's or Beth's. Maybe Beth paid more attention to her room than to her appearance. Was a crazy notion, but anything was possible. Everywhere was tidy and the space had a nice, cool air about it. The sheer, white curtains had certainly added to that feel. Like the first room, no one was in there either and I didn't hear a sound. I surely hoped Rob was listening out for any movement inside the houses where he was supposed to go.

I went on each side of the house, looking in and glancing around every so often with hopes that none of the other neighbors were on to me. The end result was that no one appeared to be at home. If they were, they were probably hiding under the beds or in the closet because I surely didn't see anyone.

Walking the front strip this time, I moved on to the Coopers' little quaint dwelling that was situated in a cul-de-sac. The Coopers were a young couple that just tied the knot two years earlier. They had an infant son named Max whom they adored. From time to time, I'd see Sheila Cooper in the food store picking up things for the baby while Mr. Cooper stood nearby with Max strapped securely on his chest. They were decent people who seemed to actually like each other and I sort of admired them. When I didn't see them at the store, one of them was outdoors pushing Max in his comfy looking stroller. Max was one of those smiling babies who wanted to go to everyone. Didn't matter how the person looked or smelled. One time, he held out those little, chubby arms of his for Jase to pick him up and I was pretty sure Jase hadn't showered or anything yet for the day or for a couple of days, for that matter. Yet, he still got the girls and even the cute babies running after him. I did once consider that maybe I needed to adopt his style since he obviously had it going on, but knowing Mom, I would've been chased out of the house if I decided to neglect proper hygiene. Jase knew he couldn't come inside our house when Mom was there if he didn't look halfway decent. But he was often there like it was his second home whenever "the cat was away".

I did a careful look around the Coopers' house and quickly arrived at the conclusion that they weren't there. I couldn't see inside some of the windows, but I was able to get a good view past a few. Just to make sure, I even knocked at their back door to see if anyone would answer.

Nope. Not a word. They, too, were off somewhere and the question running through my mind right then was: *Where were they and where were the Washingtons and Sam's folks?*

When I got back to Sam's house, Rob was already there. He and Sam were sitting in the living room.

"Any luck?" Rob asked the moment I walked through the door.

I shook my head. "Nope. You?"

"Nope," he answered.

Sam looked more worried than before. "It can't all be a coincidence, can it?" she asked.

I sat down with them. "I doubt it. None of these people had dogs, yet they're gone." Then I started to think deeper. "Well, to be fair guys… just because those neighbors weren't at home when we checked doesn't mean something happened to them."

"I think it does if all the cars are still parked in their yards," Sam replied. "Were the cars there?" She glanced at Rob and me.

We both nodded.

"You're right," I said. "I forgot about that very important detail."

"Yeah. I doubt they all went for a neighborhood stroll," Rob commented.

Those awful dogs must've done something to them!" Sam cried.

"Let's not jump to any conclusions," I calmly said.

And it was the first time I'd ever seen such a glare coming my way from Sam's eyes.

"Jump to conclusions?" she snarled. "Are you in denial, Hewey Spader? My parents and the others are gone! Are you blind or stupid?"

Rob looked quite startled. He was used to Sam verbally bashing him whenever he managed to get on her nerves, but she was usually far more patient with me. I guess there's a first time for everything.

"Hey guys…" Rob suddenly had a very worried look on his face. "If Sam's folks and some of the other neighbors around here have upped and disappeared, I wonder if my folks are still around."

"That's a good point," I said. "Now's a good time as any to check."

We'd have to go around the bend and further up the road to get to Rob's house.

"Let's go," I said to them.

"No," Rob replied. "I think it's best I go alone this time. "You two wait here for me, okay?"

"Are you sure?" I asked.

"Yep."

He proceeded to leave.

"Please be careful," Sam told him with both hands interlocked beneath her chin.

4

Rob returned less than twenty minutes later. His folks were both at home and pretty much the same as usual—which added to the mystery as to what happened to the others. None of this was making sense, considering that it was publicly announced, in so many words, that only people whose dogs no longer wanted them around were the ones who'd be shipped out.

Sam had taken a quick shower and a change of clothes while Rob was gone. "I'm glad your peeps are all right," she told him.

Sam looked rather distressed as she sat alone on the couch. I was still standing near the door after letting Rob in. He'd gone over to the sofa and put his feet up.

"Get your dirty shoes off that chair!" Sam barked.

He immediately obeyed. Sometimes, Rob did the dumbest things. Everyone knew how Sam and her folks were when it came to certain conduct, and putting one's feet up in any of the chairs, especially with shoes on, was completely out of the question.

"Oh, sorry! I forgot," he blurted. Then he looked at me. "So, what now?"

I started back over to the couch when my cell vibrated. Quickly, I slid it out of my blue jeans pocket and noticed the call was coming from a private number.

"Hello..."

"It's me. Where are you?" I recognized Jeffrey's voice right away.

"At Sam's place," I said.

"Meet me down the road. You know where. Same as last time."

"Okay. Leaving now."

"It's Jeffreys," I told Sam and Rob who'd been staring me down the entire conversation. "We gotta go."

"Where?" Rob asked.

"The spot. Gotta leave now."

Sam secured the house and brought the front door key with her. During the walk back, we barely spoke a word to each other. I suppose all of our minds were consumed with thoughts of what Jeffreys and Hugo might reveal. Sam suddenly found herself in the same situation as I was—not knowing where her family was, so I knew firsthand how she felt.

We noticed the area in vicinity of my house was vastly different from the street Sam's house was on. There was little activity at a few residences here and there as we continued along. However, Sam's road was more like a ghost town.

We met Jeffreys waiting on the step in front of the back door, which was well out of view. He seemed a bit nervous, though it was evident to me that he was trying to hide it. The moment we got inside, he pulled out a cigarette and lit it with his lighter.

"Let's go upstairs," I said. "We can talk more freely and won't have to worry about being heard if anyone happened to pass by."

"Good idea," he replied.

"Where's Hugo?" Sam asked.

"He's at home. He thought it best I meet with you all alone this time. We have to be so careful."

"I know what you mean," Sam said.

When we got upstairs, Jeffreys took the same seat he had the last time. Sam and I sat on the bench together and Rob stood near the doorway.

"Have you found out anything?" I asked, eagerly.

He nodded and took a puff. "Why else do you think I'm here?"

He had a point. Guess it was a stupid question when you really think about it.

He crossed his legs and looked me dead in the eyes. "I know where they took your family," he said.

I slid more towards the edge of the bench. "Really? Where?"

"They're being held in that new facility the government's been building for the past two years. I don't know if you knew about it, but it's way out in the western end of town. Huge place. Rumor has it they were setting up some sort of military base or something. Not sure though."

"Okay... I think I heard about it. So, can you take us there? Sam's family are also missing. We just found out today. Maybe they're there too?"

He shrugged. "It's a possibility. According to Hugo, a lot more's going on than what those in charge decided they'd share with us. As for taking *us* anywhere, that's not gonna work."

"Why not?" I was puzzled.

He leaned forward slightly. "Look, I told you the last time I was here that if we're going to do anything, we need to have a plan. You can't possibly think we can just drive up there, grab your family members and leave without finding ourselves staring at the business end of a possibly very big gun. Or even worse—getting chewed alive by some dangerous canines who happen to be currently acting like humans."

"Okay. So, how can we take care of this?" I asked him.

I heard all of his talk of a *plan*, but I was thinking beyond that. I just needed to get there and would've figured everything out afterwards. I told you that was usually my MO.

"First of all, regardless of who else's parents have gone missing, there'll be no *we*?"

"What do you mean by that, Jeffreys?" Sam seemed very offended.

He looked at her. "Hugo and I have spent a lot of time thinking this thing through ever since he got word of where people were being held. Spader will be the only one going out there with us as we can't afford to take reckless chances. It's very dangerous."

He turned to me again. "And you'll have to travel in the trunk."

I didn't care if he said I'd be tied underneath the car, I just wanted to get there. "Fine. When do we do this?" I asked.

"Hugo has to go to the facility, now known as their headquarters to meet his commander early tomorrow morning. You'll come along with us," Jeffreys replied.

"So, how do we get them out? Does Hugo have access to any weapons in case we need them?"

"You won't be getting your family out tomorrow," he said. "You're only going along to see what we're facing and then we all will decide the best way to proceed."

"I got what you're saying," Sam chimed in. "You'll be like staking out."

"Precisely!" Jeffreys exclaimed as if it was the first sensible thing he'd heard for the day.

"And after y'all see what's happening, y'all will go in there and get Hewey's peeps and mine."

"We'll rescue your peeps," Jeffreys replied with a tinge of sarcasm.

Sam seemed satisfied. I guess as far as she was concerned, any plan was better than none at all.

Rob took a seat on the floor. "But how will Hewey get to see anything if he'll be stuck in the trunk?"

"Good question," I added, looking at Jeffreys.

"You'll get to see what you need to; trust me," Jeffreys told me.

"So, has anyone thought about how we'll get out of town once they've been rescued?" Rob asked.

"Believe me, young man... Hugo has got a plan that just might stop all this madness and hopefully, change things to the way they were before."

"Really?" Rob's eyes widened.

"Yup. We all have to pray it works."

Jeffreys didn't stay at the distillery a minute longer than he deemed necessary. He told me what time he'd pick me up the next day and I couldn't wait for dawn to come.

5

Shortly after 6:00 A.M., Jeffreys pulled up at the rear of the distillery. He'd called my cell and allowed it to ring once before hanging up. As discussed the previous day, that was the signal he'd use to let me know he was outside. I was wide awake and dressed from 4:00 A.M., so in a flash I was downstairs. Rob locked the door of the distillery behind me.

Jeffreys was standing next to his twenty-year-old Chevy sedan and he opened the back door directly behind the driver's seat and gestured for me to get in. However, I noticed the seat adjacent to the trunk was lying down flat and I could see the inside of the trunk. It wasn't so small in that I knew I could fit in there rather comfortably. If he ever kept anything in there, it was all cleared out now.

"Should I go in the trunk now?" I asked.

"Yup. We'll keep the seat down until we're almost there, before sealing you off," Jeffreys replied.

Hugo was in the front passenger seat looking spiffy in his military uniform. He even had dark green and silver semi-rectangular stripes on his sleeves.

"A wonderful day to you, young man," Hugo said.

I nodded to him as I made my way into the trunk, figuring Jeffreys had me get in that way instead of the normal way so I'll know how to maneuver later. Moments later, we were off.

I could feel every dent and bump in the road during the long drive. Jeffreys' car was obviously in dire need of new shock absorbers, among other improvements. I guess the best improvement would've been for him to finally get rid of that old car and invest in something new. Jeffreys was a miser though; saved every dime possible as if all of it was going with him in the grave. The house he was living in had been passed down to him from his parents, and he never knew what it was to find money to pay for a mortgage, unlike my folks. Other than having Hugo around, he didn't have a wife or children—no one else to care for except, of course, his beloved dog.

Lying in a fetal position in the trunk, I just imagined how fat Jeffreys' bank account was. I never could figure people like him out. I'd met some folks over the years that were very stingy, but they spared no expense when it came to getting stuff for themselves. Not Jeffreys though. I'm sure, in his mind, that money was always better off right where it was in that local bank downtown. He was bound to ride that Chevy into the ground before he paid a penny for a new ride.

I heard him and Hugo engaged in conversation part of the way. Hugo spoke very intelligently and conducted himself like a real gentleman—I guess it would be *gentledog*. He had a rather calm, cool and collected demeanor; didn't seem to be bothered by much. Apparently, he brought some balance to Jeffreys' life although Jeffrey wasn't radically different. Jeffreys could be a major pain in the butt though, so it took a special dog to care to be around him. Maybe he was like that because he'd had it so good and was a spoiled brat. I arrived at that conclusion when I visited ninety-year-old Ms. Dottie Pearl one day, who was Jeffreys' next door neighbor and had been friendly with his folks when they were still alive. Ms. Pearl often had me come over to help her change a light bulb or do some odds and ends around the yard. She confessed she didn't like *the boy* because he was a spoiled rascal; got what he wanted most times and threw a devilish tantrum when he didn't. Inwardly, she blamed Jeffreys for his folks' eventual illnesses—Mae Jeffreys came down with a stroke while Ed battled a heart condition. She said she listened from her li'l house as Jeffreys complained about this or that from the time he was a young man straight up until Mae had another stroke and ended up in a nursing home. She was only there for six months before she died and poor Ed escaped to the *sweet by and by* one night in the middle of his sleep. I'd asked her what Jeffreys always created the upset about and she said it ranged from any li'l senseless thing to some land he wanted them to turn over to him early so he could sell it and wouldn't have to work for that marketing firm he'd been employed with. Mae and Ed wanted to hold on to the land in case they needed it, but Jeffreys was insistent that they were denying him his inheritance because they were mean and didn't want to see him have it easy. The way Ms. Pearl spoke, sounded like Jeffreys was a real scrooge and manipulator too. After she enlightened me with his business, I took pleasure egging his house, along with the guys, every so often. To me, it was payback on behalf of his folks and Ms. Pearl too. Ms. Pearl had made it to ninety-seven before her eyes closed for good.

"Hey! Spader!" I heard Jeffreys say.

"Yeah," I answered.

"We're almost there. In the center of the back seat, there's a short rope. Once you pull on it, it'll seal off the trunk. Later, when I give the seat a li'l knock, that's your cue to open the latch and crawl out, but stay down when you do. Got it?"

"Okay."

"Don't move a muscle and if you've gotta sneeze or cough, find a way to keep it in. One wrong move and we're all in deep trouble. Got it?"

"I do," I replied.

"Okay. Pull up the seat and keep quiet."

I had to give the seat a good yank, but it landed right in place and I was suddenly plunged into vehicular darkness.

We drove a while further before I felt us going over a couple of speed bumps, then the vehicle slowed to a complete stop.

"I'm here to meet with the commander," Hugo told someone. I presumed we were at a security check point.

I heard the light clashing of metal and then a rolling sound. That must've been a gate. Shortly thereafter, the car was moving again.

"Just passed security," Jeffreys indicated, moments later. "Driving up to the front of the main building. Hugo will get out here, then I'll go and park."

I didn't respond, specifically since he didn't give me previous instructions that I should. I wasn't about to do anything that could potentially jack up our plans. We'd come too far for that.

About a minute later, the car slowed again. I heard a door open, then shut. I presumed Hugo had left the vehicle. After that, we were moving again, but at an even slower pace.

"Parking now," Jeffreys said.

I could tell that he was pulling into a spot, then we stopped completely and he shut the engine off.

"You can push the seat back down," he said. "But don't come out until I tell you." I guess just speaking his wishes instead of leaning back and knocking the seat like he said he would've made more sense.

I followed his instructions and was relieved to see the light of day again. We were parked facing the east and directly under the shade of a large tree.

"The coast is clear. You can ease out and have a quick look; just keep your head lowered," Jeffreys spoke quietly.

I crawled out of the trunk and stooping low from the back seat, I looked through the window on my right. The compound we were on was huge! The ground was compacted dirt mainly—that stage right before an area is paved. Throughout the compound were several buildings and at each side of the front entrances that were visible to me were either a couple of guard dogs or armed men. One of the buildings looked like a large office space with a double door entrance while the other three resembled long, rectangular warehouses. I noticed a few people and dogs walking from the main building to their vehicles, and others from one building to the next. They all appeared to work there or at least for *them*. A chain-link fence with barbed wire on top surrounded the property and I couldn't help thinking that whatever the government had initially designed this compound for it was likely to have been for something major. Now, the canines had taken it over for whatever purpose they had in mind. I noticed seven or eight large, yellow buses parked along the southern side of the fence, a good distance away from the main section of the parking lot.

Jeffreys had made a smart move when he pulled up in that particular spot as we were primarily away from where the other vehicles were situated, yet not too far from what I deemed the office building.

"Hugo went in the one directly behind us," Jeffreys told me, as he stared through his rear-view mirror.

"Did you see anyone when you drove into this place?" I loudly whispered.

"You mean like anyone you know?" he asked.

"Yeah."

"No, I didn't. This is Hugo's first time here too. Let's just wait and see what he says, shall we?"

I nodded.

"The good thing is he'd be able to see what the setup's like and what we'd be facing."

"I understand."

Other than for a little foot traffic in the parking lot, there wasn't much of anything going on from what I could see. Peering further back, I noticed the security booth we would've passed to get in. I noticed a couple of heads through the glass window of the booth and two armed men and a bad-looking uniformed Boerboel standing with them.

"I see Hugo." Jeffreys was still looking through the rear-view mirror. "He's walking over toward another building. Someone's with him."

I carefully peeped through the back window and saw him with another dog—a Rottweiler.

"Is that his commander?" I asked.

"Yep. That's him, all right."

I must confess, they both looked rather spiffy in those uniforms. I was still getting used to their human-like behavior.

"I wonder what they're doing."

He sighed. "We'll find out soon enough."

For the next few minutes, I studied the surroundings with an attempt to keep everything in my head for when it was time to come back again. I'd watched enough spy movies to know familiarizing yourself with enemy territory gave you the advantage. Sam would've totally agreed.

"Get down!" Jeffreys yelled.

Hugo was approaching the car along with his commander. "Get in the trunk now and close it. Hurry!"

He didn't have to tell me twice. I was in there in a flash, tucked away nice and neat.

I barely heard the canine instructing Jeffreys on where to go and wasn't sure what he was talking about. Jeffreys only said: "Yes, sir," and I'm sure he was putting on the act that would protect his very life and freedom. A minute later, I heard the car door squeak open, then shut again. The engine switched on and we were in reverse mode.

Hugo and Jeffreys were silent as we drove. It seemed like we were heading in a different direction from where we came as the ride was a bit rougher and it felt like we were rolling over rocky surface. I figured it must've been the way to exit the compound although I'd clearly seen an exit lane at the security gate when I peeked back at it.

We were driving for approximately three minutes before the car slowed and then came to a halt. I wondered where we were and what the reason was for us stopping.

The car door opened and shut again. Then I heard Jeffreys calling me. "Come out," he said, "and stay down. You need to see this."

I gently pushed out the back and crawled out on top of the flattened seat. Jeffreys turned his head slightly to the right, his eyes darting around. "You're not gonna believe this, Spader" he said.

"What?" I asked.

"Look over to your right, but for goodness sake, keep your head low!" He whispered loudly, barely moving his lips.

I eased up slightly and immediately, was horrified at what I saw. Scores of people were inside a large, fenced-in area with pickaxes or shovels in hand, digging a massive, oval pit. Uniformed canines were on guard duty there and instructing the workers. It was evident to me that the project was specifically laid out where workers were standing at the spot they were to start digging from, moving inward as they go, perhaps depending on if they'd dug deeply enough from the edges. That is how I was able to see the actual width of the pit that they were digging. At least two hundred people were out there in the hot sun—men, women and teenage children. What absolutely sickened me was the fact that my folks and Carl were among the workers and so were Uncle Charlie, Jase and his mom, Sam's folks, the Washingtons, Mr. Cooper from Sam's corner, and others who'd suddenly gone missing from their homes. I assumed Mrs. Cooper was indoors with their baby.

"Mom! Dad!" I quietly whispered. I was heartbroken and angry, fighting the urge to run over to them. "What're they making them do?" I asked Jeffreys.

He pressed his lips. "I have an idea, but don't want to jump to any conclusions. Hugo might have the answer to that question."

Hugo was having a conversation with two big mastiffs who were wearing a slightly different uniform from the others. The others wore a teal-colored uniform when theirs was a light brown.

"Is this supposed to be prison?" I blurted, angrily. "What the hell do they think they're doing?"

"I know it's hard, but stay cool," Jeffreys said. "At least we know where they are and can set some sort of plan in motion."

Hearing him speak confidently about rescuing my folks made me feel a little better, in spite of the atrocity I was witnessing with my own eyes. Mom was in no condition to do any hard labor and neither was Carl. Dad was strong, but he wasn't used to that kind of work. And the Washingtons and other elderly folks weren't strong or healthy enough to endure such harsh treatment.

I sighed heavily. "Whatever we come up with, we have to do it right away. A lot of these people can't survive this heat, let alone hard labor."

Hugo headed back to the car and I returned to the hiding spot, pulling the seat up again. I was dying to know what Hugo found out and realized I'd have to wait until we were out of there.

As I lay crouched in darkness, different scenarios played in my head as to how we'd rescue my folks and Sam's too, as well as Jase and his mom, and Uncle Charlie. Ultimately, I wondered if it would take a miracle to do what seemed like the impossible.

6

After we had left the compound, I pushed open the back seat again and listened as Hugo explained exactly what was going on. I would've never imagined any of it in a million years.

"I will be working at the compound starting tomorrow," he told us. "The commander wanted to show me around and inform me of my duties ahead of time in person since he won't be there in the morning when I arrive." He glanced back at me. "I know that doesn't interest you in the least bit, so let me get to the nitty-gritty." He paused.

"The long and short of it is that they're digging a mass grave and I'm not aware if those who are put to toil recognize that a special spot is reserved for them—eventually, anyway.

"You mean...the dogs plan to murder everyone?" I was stunned.

"Not everyone. Just the people who are dispensable. Basically, those people who were transported here and others who may end up here."

"That's terrible!" Jeffreys glanced at him.

"Why would they want to do that?" I asked.

"What you don't understand, young man, is that their actions are not without reason. They're here in a domineering position in the first place because humans have proven that they don't usually handle power all that well. Remember, I said this was payback?"

"Yeah." I nodded.

"Well, it's more than just that. Many humans have not only been unfair and unkind to animals; they've also been unfair and unkind to each other. Canines now have a mission in

Eppington to restore order and to—pardon my expression—*clean up shop*." He shifted slightly toward me in his chair. "It's almost like when you've been given something of value and you either don't use it or you misuse it, then it's taken away from you and given to someone else—in this case, *us*. Humans were given a huge, yet straightforward responsibility to put the intelligence they have been given to good use. Instead, many have acted like beasts who weren't given the ability to reason, make sensible decisions and respect one another and their property. For a long time, we, the canines, have been seemingly at odds with felines, for instance. That's because we weren't afforded the same skills you were given to comprehend the concept of harmonious living, conflict resolution, etcetera, etcetera... However, now the intelligence has been transferred to us, leaving humans in a daze-like, subservient position and I must confess, we're doing a better job already. You don't see us gossiping and back-biting, stealing, killing each other like one of you went and did to that poor lady who lived just down the street from you."

"You know about Mrs. Christie?" I asked.

"We all do." He arched an eyebrow. "But you should ask... Are we investigating her murder? And the answer is currently *no*. She is one of you. It should've never happened. Our focus is on transforming this town into the kind of place it should be and to do the same in every town around the globe that must be revamped. Have I explained myself clearly, thus far?"

As I listened to Hugo, I found myself becoming extremely annoyed, even though I couldn't deny that many of his points were valid.

"I hear you, Hugo, but the fact that canines are willing to slaughter human beings like other human beings have done to each other ages ago makes them no better than we are."

"I second that!" Jeffreys exclaimed, keeping his eyes on the road.

"But indeed this is different, if I do say so myself!" Hugo asserted. "Motivation for such atrocities in human history was fueled by hatred, racism and a twisted sense of superiority. Canines are not getting rid of people for any of those horrid reasons. It is simply to create a new beginning, a new town, a new atmosphere—one filled with love and respect for one another. It is to create a place where children and pups can grow up and safely walk the streets; where canines and humans can sleep with their houses unlocked and assist each other in this here community. Nothing done is accredited with any type of cruel or evil intent and although I don't fully subscribe to this new norm, I certainly understand it. Don't get me wrong…" he raised a paw, "I am not in support of anyone being killed. Not at all. I personally don't think any reason is good enough for snuffing out anyone's life, unless it's in self-defense, of course. I am only explaining the reasoning behind what is happening here."

"So, how can we stop them?" I asked. "We can't sit by and let them do this! It's not just about my folks or Sam's—it's about the lives of so many other innocent people too. But if all we can do is rescue our folks and figure out what to do afterwards, then I understand."

"You're thinking wisely," Hugo said.

"So, can you get your hands on guns or some other weapons we can use to go in there with?" I asked.

Hugo cleared his throat. "If my gut feeling is right, we wouldn't need guns, just a couple of strong dog chains and some supplies from a vet clinic."

"What?" Jeffreys and I said, simultaneously.

"Hugo, what on earth are you talking about?" Jeffreys grimaced.

"My dear, master. We shall have a good, long conversation later, but for now, let's head to any vet clinic and then to the hardware store before dropping the young man back off to his hiding place."

The entire time while they ran their errands, I was worried out of my mind and perplexed by Hugo's assertion that no weapons would be needed. How were we supposed to go against an army of dogs and subservient humans who'd likely shoot and kill if they were told to? I felt more confused than before, maybe because I saw what we were facing and couldn't come up with any safe way to deal with any of it. As absurd as what Hugo said sounded about vet supplies and chains, I didn't have much of a choice. I either had to trust him or don't.

Before dropping me off behind the distillery, they both agreed that the guys and I should lay low until we heard from them again. Hugo was adamant that it wouldn't take more than two days before they were in touch again.

Sam opened the door for me and I couldn't wait to get upstairs and tell them exactly what it was we were facing.

7

"I can't believe they picked up my peeps and have them over in some yard doing hard labor! And even worse, digging a grave for everybody!" Sam snarled. "They've gotta be out of their damn minds. I'm ready to go in there now and show them who's boss!"

"That's a messed up deal." Rob shook his head slowly. "This whole thing has gone from bad to worse."

"Well, they started it and I'm gonna finish it!" she returned.

It was the next morning and Sam, Rob and I had stayed up most of the night talking about the compound and what was going on there. After we woke up, it was no different. I'm quite sure I even dreamed of that huge pit the night before.

"Jeffreys and Hugo had better get back to us soon because this crap has got to stop!" Sam exclaimed. "Chains and vet supplies? Are you kidding? How the hell are those things supposed to help in rescuing our peeps?"

"I have no idea." I shook my head. "I hope Hugo knows what he's doing."

"Anybody have a better plan?" Rob asked.

"Well, we don't know what Hugo's plans are, but my plan would be to gather as much ammo as possible, march in there and take over the place," Sam said.

"Easier said than done, although that would've been my number one move," I replied. "Who knows if we'd accomplish anything or even come out alive? But anything's worth a shot."

"Yep." Rob reached for the loaf of bread and the peanut butter. We'd cleared and dusted off a shelf near the doorway and placed the food on top, hoping no roaches would get any of it.

"They're not investigating Mrs. Christie's murder, so it looks like the killer is bound to get away with it," I told them.

"Maybe one of *them* did it," Sam suggested.

"I doubt that." I got up from my mat and headed toward the bathroom. "That doesn't seem to be their style."

"But wiping out dozens of people at once is more like it, huh?"

"Don't know. Gotta take a leak."

* * * *

Rob handed me my cell that had gone off after I stepped out of the bathroom.

"It's Jeffreys," he said.

"Hey, Jeffreys…" I answered, eagerly.

"We're coming by soon, so make sure the door downstairs is unlocked. No need to come down; I'll lock it behind us."

"Okay," I said.

"I knew from the sound of his voice that they had a plan in mind for us to rescue my folks and I was anxious to hear how they thought we ought to go about it.

"They're on their way here!" I told the guys, excitedly.

Sam was still lying on her mat and looked like she'd had a rough night. Rob was sitting in a chair fiddling with his cell.

"I'd better get myself together." Sam got up and placed her mat against the side of the wall, then grabbed a pair of shorts and a cotton shirt from her bag and headed into the bathroom. She then looked back at me. "Before I go in there, did you put down the lid, Hewey?"

"Don't I always?" I frowned.

"Not last night, you didn't."

"How do you know it was me?"

"Who else would it be?" Rob interjected.

I shook my head and Sam went into the bathroom.

"I'll go unlock the door," I told Rob. "They'll be here soon. He's gonna lock the door behind them after they get in."

"Cool," Rob replied.

I went downstairs, removed the two-by-four from across the door and unlocked the latch. Then I jogged back upstairs.

"I could sure use some hot chocolate," Rob said.

"I could use a strong cup of coffee or even better, some of that wine my dad sipped on most evenings."

As I combed my fingers through my hair, I felt a deep sigh escape. For me, all of this was just the beginning and what we were about to discuss there in that room, once implemented, would affect each of us in a major way—hopefully, positively.

I sauntered over to the bench and sat down, then looked aimlessly out of window at our neighborhood. I'd seen Julio Perez on the government compound working his butt off in the scorching heat. I guess he deserved it for the way he treated his next-door neighbors, the Riveras. In fact, he deserved worse than that, but the old goat didn't deserve to die; certainly not in the way the canines had in mind for his demise. As much of a turn off as Julio was, I knew if I had the opportunity to help him, I would. My folks taught me to not allow my feelings about people to prevent me from doing the right thing whenever the opportunity presented itself. I wasn't totally ignoring them when they spoke. I think they would've been pleased to know I'd listened to at least something they'd tried to drill into my head. Would Julio have done the same for me? I doubt it. I truly didn't believe the old timer had a decent bone in his body, but who was I to judge?

"It's do or die now, huh?" Rob looked at me as I sat alone, in deep contemplation.

I nodded. "Yep. Do or die."

We sat in silence for about a good minute, then I said, "You know, bud, I wanna say that I really appreciate you supporting Sam and me in getting our folks back. I mean...you could say even right now that you don't want any part of possibly risking your life when your folks are safe at home."

"Are you crazy, Hewey?" He grimaced.

"Uh?" I was confused for a second there.

"My folks could be next! It would be silly of me to think they're in the clear just because they're still at the house. Besides... no matter what, I couldn't abandon my friends. Jase is out there too. All for one and one for all, right?"

"Right." I smiled.

I heard the back door slam and at that moment, Sam exited the bathroom, then came over and stood next to me. None of us moved a muscle or said a word as we heard the footsteps heading up the staircase towards us. Jeffreys and Hugo were finally here to reveal what they thought would work to accomplish our mission.

I knew I had the best friends a kid could ever ask for. Sam and Rob were fearless, in my opinion (even though I'd just in the past week started witnessing Rob's courage). Our guests were almost at the top landing and Sam and I glanced at each other in anticipation. That girl was ready as ready could be—all of us were. This was a *war* and with the ramifications of such clear in our heads, there was no way we'd be backing down. Too much was at stake.

The footsteps sounded odd—in that one might've thought if he didn't know better that there were more than just a man and his dog coming to meet us and one, like me, would've been shocked to find two very large canines at the top landing walking through our door on all fours, then swiftly standing on their hind legs. The canines were dressed in those light brown military uniforms like what I'd seen those guards in at the government compound. In fact, I realized that those dogs were the same two Hugo had been speaking with at what would be the mass gravesite while Jeffreys and I waited in the car. This couldn't be happening... What on earth were they doing in our spot?

The look on Sam's and Rob's faces was one that I'd never forgotten all these years later. They looked like they'd seen a ghost and I can only imagine the expression my face held which was forever embedded into their minds. I started to get up and Rob stood to his feet immediately.

"So, this is where some teenage brats have hidden all this time..." One of the dogs walked slowly and arrogantly around the room, passing the three of us with a reprimanding gaze.

"What is this?" I asked, boldly, yet with cloaked timidity. "What're you doing here and what do you want?"

"Don't look in their eyes!" Sam warned me.

The other dog waited just past the doorway, nearby where Rob was standing nervously.

"I see. That's been your strategy, huh?" The dog who'd spoken before remarked. "By the way, in spite of everything, there's no need for us all to remain strangers. My name is Brick and this here..." he gestured, "...is my brother, Dutch. Our father is who you know as simply *Leader*."

The guys and I instantly glanced at each other. We knew these canines were at the highest level of this blasted conspiracy to take over our town and to eliminate our families.

"We're not afraid of you," I charged. "You're a bunch of four-legged bullies who think you're better than everyone in this town.

Well, you're not gonna stop us. You'd have to chew us to pieces first!"

I happened to glance at Rob after I'd said that and noticed the clear fright on his face. Certainly, none of us wanted to be chewed to bits, but I had to say something to show we weren't any pushovers. I knew well enough that the only way to not become hopeless victims was to stand up to bullies. Worked every time for me throughout middle school and even if it didn't work right then and there, it was worth a try.

"I second that!" Sam blurted, nodding at me approvingly.

"Yeah. Me too!" Rob chimed in.

"I must confess... they've got guts," Dutch said with a sinister smile on his rugged face.

Brick grinned. "They do. I'm thinking they'd be perfect in the military once they'd been properly programmed. Maybe we won't give them the full effect, but should keep them with some sense of individuality. Although risky, it might benefit us even more in the long run."

"Or maybe, we should scratch all that and just dispose of them. Not such a good idea to keep troublemakers around, huh?"

Contemplatively, Brick soon replied, "You're probably right."

Just then, Jeffreys and Hugo entered the room; Hugo, walking on hind legs. They both appeared eerily calm about what was seemingly transpiring in front of them. Jeffreys' hands were inside his pockets and he and Hugo remained near the doorway, a couple of feet behind Dutch.

Brick looked at them and smiled. "You've done a wonderful job, gentlemen. You will be greatly rewarded for your efforts."

Sam nudged me.

"I knew that bastard couldn't be trusted!" she exclaimed. "I knew it from that first day he showed up here."

Rob was shaking his head, disappointingly.

"How could you do this?" I said to Jeffreys. "We depended on you to do the right thing. But you just couldn't; could you? I was right about you all along—and so was Ms. Pearl!"

He didn't respond.

"He's a punk; that's what!" Sam said. "Punks do what he did and that animal of his, to think he fooled us like that! I should've known he was no different from the rest of 'em. They all have everything to gain."

Brick made his way over to his accomplices and stood proudly next to Jeffreys. "There is nothing at all comparable to loyalty," he said. "Our father taught us that from a tender age and it's obvious to me that Hugo has done the same with this fine human as of late, who has willingly betrayed his own kind for the good of this town."

Jeffreys had stood silently all along and I wondered if cat had suddenly got his tongue in spite of the heated confrontation. Then, I saw one of his hands slip from his pocket, and Hugo was moving in closer to Dutch who was in front of him. Together, Jeffreys hand went up and Hugo's front paw, and in an instant the guys and I witnessed the most shocking thing ever since our town had been turned upside down. Jeffreys had sneakily injected something into the side of Brick's neck while Hugo injected something into Dutch's. Both canines fell to the floor seconds later like two sacks of potatoes.

Our eyes widened with astonishment as Jeffreys and Hugo stood before us with both a satisfied and nervous expression on their faces. The two brothers never saw it coming.

"No need to fear," Hugo started. "They're not dead. Just in a very deep sleep right now."

"So, you didn't betray us after all!" Sam smiled.

"Doesn't look like it, huh?" Jeffreys replied, evenly.

Rob advanced a little closer toward the sleeping dogs. "Serves 'em right."

"So, what now?" I asked Jeffreys and Hugo.

"We have some chains in the car and a chair. It would be great if two of you will go down and get them. They're in the trunk. The car's unlocked," Jeffreys said.

"I'll go," Rob offered.

"I'll come with you." Sam eagerly joined him.

"You really had us all fooled for a minute there." I walked over to him. "Why didn't you tell me what was going to happen?"

"I wanted to, but Hugo and I felt it would be too risky. We needed your reaction to them being here to be as genuine as humanly possible so that when we made our move, it would be seamless. And so, it was." He nodded.

"So, what do we do now?" I asked.

"We chain them, videotape them and send the recording to Leader—their father," Hugo answered.

Sam and Rob walked in with the chains as Hugo was explaining.

"What will keeping them here do to help get our peeps out?" Sam asked, handing the chain to Jeffreys.

Rob rested the iron chair and the chain he was carrying on the floor a couple of feet away from Brick. The chair looked like one you would've found in many of the houses in our neighborhood. It was a simple dining room chair.

"Oh! I got it!" Sam exclaimed. "You're setting up an exchange. The leader's sons, I guess you could call them…for our peeps."

"Not quite," Hugo replied, much to Sam's surprise. It was obvious she thought she had it all figured out.

"If my assumption is correct, Leader's loyalty to his sons is paramount and if we are able to twist his hand a good bit, their confinement may be the thing that turns everything around in this town. If we play our cards right, of course."

I didn't get a full explanation, but figured if anyone in that room knew those canines for what they were, it would be Hugo. And it would be Hugo that would give us the best shot at hitting them where it hurts.

"Anything you say," I replied.

"Yeah. We're in," Sam said, after glancing at Rob.

"Well then, grab that chair from over there, young man, along with this one you just brought up," Hugo said to Rob. "And let's get these two officers up and seated. They're about to make their television debut."

8

Brick and Dutch were each confined to a chair. We were careful to ensure that when they happened to wake up, they wouldn't be able to fight their way out of them. The chain was placed on them starting from the chest area and swirling around the chair several times until their body was properly restrained. We all worked as a team—Hugo, being the instructor as to how things must be done.

Jeffreys moved the bench away from the window and set up a camera he'd also brought along in the car to face the sleeping canine giants. It was decided I would be the one to speak and no one else except for me, Brick and Dutch would be visible in the background. Hugo said it would be obvious to the leader that I hadn't taken down two of his canines by myself and it would have him wondering how many of us were wandering around with our perfect senses, prepared to wage war against them. I thought it was a plan of pure ingenuity. I just hoped in the end, everything would turn out the way Hugo thought it might. He was still privy to something we couldn't quite comprehend.

I stood behind the restrained, sleeping dogs as Jeffreys and Hugo had instructed and I sent a clear, concise message to their father concerning his sons' captivity and what was coming next for them if he didn't agree to allow me safe entry into the compound right away along with a few friends, and subsequently meet our demands. The recording was no more than three minutes long and after that, with a click of a button, Jeffreys sent it as an email attachment to the leader. Hugo had access to the leader's private email address and his cell phone. His internet access did not go beyond Eppington's perimeter. These dogs were certainly taking over. I was stunned to know that they were just as technically savvy as many humans were and even more organized than most.

"There it is," Hugo said with a yawn. "Now, we just wait."

Jeffreys had created a new email address so that the leader would not automatically figure out who had sent the message. My involvement in this matter was not a secret, but theirs was for the time being.

Within five minutes, a notification went off on Hugo's phone that Jeffreys was holding.

"It's him!" Jeffreys said, peering down at the small lettering. "He's agreed to meet right away and promised we have immediate clearance to enter the compound.

"Yay!" Sam jumped and clapped, then hugged me. Rob was smiling from ear to ear.

Then I think the reality of what was coming next hit Sam like a ton of bricks.

"This means you're going without us?" She asked, knowingly.

I nodded. "I have to. You and Rob have to stay here with these two brutes." I was hoping to make her laugh.

"We're still in this together even though it seems like I'm entering the lions' den without you guys," I added.

I could sense her reluctance to see me go.

"Just do what Jeffreys and Hugo said to do if these dogs show the slightest sign of waking up."

"Yeah. Stick 'em again!" Rob boldly announced. He had the syringes in his pockets for safekeeping.

"Those two are not likely to wake up for hours, so we might very well be back by then."

"Yeah...*might*," Sam said.

"We will," I told her, looking into those beautiful eyes of hers.

"But what if you don't come back?" She asked. "What are we supposed to do and with these two?"

There was a brief period of memorable silence.

"You will know, my dear," Hugo said. "You have a natural instinct to survive."

I knew my friends had to take those words for what they were worth. It wasn't like they had much of a choice otherwise.

I gave Sam the tightest hug I think I'd ever given her before and shook Rob's hands briskly. He and I were teenagers, but in our minds, we were grown men—if not before, then at that moment in time.

"Take care of Sam 'til I get back," I told him.

He gave me a military salute with an assuring smile, then Jeffreys, Hugo and I headed out to the car.

We were on our way to the compound.

9

Asking Rob to take care of Sam was a tall order, particularly when I knew she was tougher than he was. Nevertheless, she was a girl—*excuse me*—a lady, despite the fact she rarely ever acted like it other than when she expressed concern about me, for one reason or the other.

This time, I didn't have to crouch down in the trunk, but sat with some dignity in the back seat behind Jeffreys as we took the same route we'd travelled together a couple of days earlier.

"You're a brave young man," Hugo said to me from the front passenger seat. "I assume most other people your age would not have opted to risk their life for the people they love."

"It may surprise you, Hugo, but I know a number of people who would've done the same thing that I'm doing. We're not all selfish, you know. I believe human beings have the innate ability to genuinely love one another and to show it just like canines can. This town may have some shady, unkind people in it just like every town does, but there are a lot of good people here too."

Jeffreys glanced at me through the rearview mirror a few times as Hugo and I conversed.

"Well, I suppose your deep commitment toward others will be obvious by the one who's capable of granting you the one wish you so desire," Hugo remarked. "I'm rooting for you."

"I am too," Jeffreys said.

"Thanks, guys. I appreciate that," I replied.

It seemed like the drive to the compound this time was quicker than the last. I wasn't sure if that was a good thing since I was nervous as hell though I believed I succeeded in not showing it. I told myself over and repeatedly "I can do this". It didn't matter if I was about to meet the leader of the canines or the leader of the free world. I had a mission which required entering enemy territory and at my young age I had enough sense to know there was a greater chance of *strength and determination* helping you when weakness would only kill you.

We slowed down to a complete halt at the security gate where a fierce-looking canine gestured for us to continue along after I'd indicated, without making eye contact, that I was there to see their leader. I saw that he had a screenshot of me in his paw and also noticed he gave Jeffreys and Hugo a somewhat condescending look.

At the distillery, I was under the impression for a while that Jeffreys and Hugo would've stayed out of sight, particularly when I was instructed to make the video solo. The question about how I'd do it all alone did cross my mind, but before I'd bothered to ask, I realized the plan consisted of stages. This planning thing was something I wasn't used to at all, as I once indicated. So, to think there would be actual parts or stages to a particular plan was like me studying physics. It was mind-boggling. Thankfully, I had pretty good guidance that hopefully, wouldn't get us killed, as well as everyone else held on that compound.

I realized Jeffreys and Hugo had taken a huge risk by getting directly involved; especially Hugo. It didn't take a rocket scientist to tell me that he'd be labeled and treated as a traitor by those who looked like him. He was a part of their military, for goodness sake! What's worse than a soldier being a traitor? Yet, he boldly came along with me like the fine canine that he was. And

Jeffreys, whom I never thought too kindly of before all this stuff happened—spoiled, self-centered Jeffreys—surprised me by risking all that he held near and dear which was largely *himself*.

Jeffreys and Hugo decided we'd drive straight around to where the pit was first to see what progress had been made. To our surprise, work on it had seemingly been halted, though we had no idea for how long. The image of my folks working out there like slaves was embedded in my mind even as we sat there for a minute with the engine running, looking over at the pit.

"I wonder why they let them do all that digging," I said. "They could've easily gotten a backhoe or something like that to do the job."

"They're aware that heavy equipment would've been faster and easier," Hugo replied. "They were in no rush and they preferred to put the people to work. It's that simple." He looked at Jeffreys who was unusually quiet. "We'd better go now."

I could see this task was not an easy one for Hugo, but he seemed to be at peace with what he was doing. I imagined being in his shoe and betraying all the humans I knew—even though they were wrong—for the sake of the canines. I'm not sure I would've been as brave or as honorable as he was. In my opinion, Hugo was one of a kind. He certainly was no Dillinger. I'd made up my mind that if I was successful in this mission, I would have a man to dog discussion with Dillinger, face to face. He'd have to answer to me for all the crap he'd done and after that, I'd never want to see him again.

Jeffreys put the car in drive and we circled back around to what I initially thought was the main office. It was the place Hugo had entered after we'd dropped him off the first day. From what he described, it wasn't merely an office, but a prison for those condemned without a fair trial.

Jeffreys didn't bother to pull into a parking spot, but instead parked brazenly in front of the main door of the building.

"Here, we are," he said, glancing at us both. Then he focused on his dog. "I guess, all I can say is that I'm proud to have you as my friend, Hugo, and I really hope this ends well for all of us."

"I do too, my friend. However it turns out, it was all worth it, eh?"

Jeffreys smiled. "Yes indeed." He turned my way. "Spader, it's largely up to you now. We've gone over this and we're confident that you can do it. At the same time, know that we're not going to blame you if it turns out differently than we'd hoped because we know you'd done your best. I hope you're successful in getting your parents back home to safety. I sure wish mine were still around."

I was sure I saw a slight welling of tears in his eyes.

"Anyway," he cleared his throat. "You go in there and you speak from the heart. We're right behind you."

"Thanks, Jeffreys." I nodded. "I'm indebted to you both."

Hugo stepped out the car first and Jeffreys and I followed him. Two armed canine guards were on both sides of the main door just like before; they looked more like statues than dogs. Hugo told them their leader was expecting me, but it appeared from their nod, that they already knew who I was. One of them opened the door for us and Hugo allowed me to enter first.

The moment I stepped inside the facility, I was approached by another canine guard who instructed me to follow him. And about fifteen feet in, the main entryway widened on both sides, revealing rows of cells containing humans on both the northern and southern sides of the building. I was appalled as I saw people I'd known all my life sitting in chairs or lying on thin, flat beds in those cells. Some were crouched on the floor, apparently staring into space. One girl was rocking back and forth hugging her knees and humming something, yet she had no expression. They were still in their own little worlds, seemingly not bothered by the fact that they were enslaved. Then I remembered what Jeffreys had said about him knowing what was going on while dazed and not being able to express himself in the slightest. So, I knew those people must've been horrified by what had become of them.

I was gently urged by Hugo to continue walking on and as I glanced back, I noticed that two human and two canine guards were trailing behind us. Though bothered by their presence, I was more bothered by the silent terror I was witnessing as I walked along the wide corridor. I'd spotted Chief Mays' poodle, Dolly-Ann, at one point, but she'd entered one of the rooms up ahead moments later.

The place had very little lighting, so inside was fairly dark even though it was daytime. I wondered if the lighting aspect was a deliberate act designed to add a dismal effect to the atmosphere of the facility. I'd learned in history class that there was more than just physical torture inflicted on human beings in times gone by. Perpetrators knew that if they could cripple their captives mentally, they had won half the fight already.

That building was extremely long and we must've walked another two minutes before I spotted Carl standing near the steel bars, back on. Mom and Dad were sitting in iron chairs looking out toward the corridor. I stopped immediately and held onto the bars, calling to all of them. Mom and Dad seemed to look through me and Carl didn't turn around.

"Mom! Dad!" I cried again, feeling the tears sliding down my cheeks. "I know you can hear me. Carl, look at me!" I yelled.

Jeffreys placed his hand on my shoulder. "I'm sorry, Spader. They can't respond to you, remember? Let's go."

I continued holding onto the bars and couldn't care less that my face was wet with tears. "Listen to me, Mom and Dad... you too Carl and hear me good... I'm coming back for you; I promise. Trust me, okay?"

I felt again like that colossal failure I'd felt I was when all I could've done was watched when that big, yellow bus came and took away my family. I stepped away from the cell and brought up my shirt sleeves to dry my face.

"Where's your so-called leader?" I demanded of the guard who we'd been following. "Take me to him now!"

I took one last look at my folks before I focused straight ahead, wanting nothing more at that moment than to come face to face with the dog that turned our lives upside down.

10

Both human and canine guards were literally at every corner of that building and all along the main area and passageways. I saw a green door straight ahead with no signage attached to it. My best guess was that it was the office of their leader or someone else in authority. I wasn't sure why I thought that. Just a feeling I had.

I soon learned that I was right as the guard in front led us into the office after knocking one time at the door.

"You go in," Hugo said. "We'll be waiting right here."

"Okay," I replied.

The canine's revered leader was standing at the left corner of the room in front of a single window. Seeing him close up gave me a better appreciation for how large of a dog he really was. Even though I was furious at him, I was amazed by his commanding presence.

The spacious room was comprised of high backed, comfortable leather chairs, and a darkly-stained desk made of cypress wood. From the location of the window, it was clear that the office was situated at the very end of the facility. I realized that from the window, the leader was able to see the pit they'd been working on which was slightly ahead and over to the right. I could see it from where I stood after I'd entered the room.

The Tibetan mastiff turned around and faced me. For a few moments, he was strangely silent—only stared. And I looked away from his gaze, determined not to make eye contact, which also meant I had to speak boldly if I were to get my point across.

He slowly approached his desk, then gestured for me—which I could see from my peripheral vision—to have a seat which I reluctantly did. He then sat down, facing me.

"And so, I meet with a mere child who has demanded the respect of Leader," he uttered in a deep, domineering voice. "Are my sons all right?"

"They are for now," I replied with my head still lowered. "How long they'll stay that way is completely up to you. My guys are with them waiting for the signal to inject them with a dose of euthanasia medication and with that, they'll go to sleep permanently—if you know what I mean." I paused, momentarily. "My only concern is for my family and the others you have here in captivity."

There was a slight pause in the room, then he asked, "Why do you not look at me?"

"I might be young, but I'm not stupid," I replied.

"So, that is how you and your *guys* have avoided detection…Very clever."

He got up and sauntered over to the window again on hind legs. His white uniform made him look more superior than all the other canines and humans combined. This animal had an air about him that was regal. However, he was not going to intimidate me and I was not about to show him an ounce of fear that he, in turn, could feed off of.

"Are you familiar with my breed, Mr. Spader?" He asked, with his back turned again.

"I am."

"Then you know that Tibetan mastiffs are considered as the strongest dogs in the world, which means that if that is true, I can turn around right now and slice you to pieces with my bare teeth in a matter of seconds."

I gulped. Couldn't help that, particularly since I knew what he proposed was quite true. "I don't doubt your ability to slaughter me on the spot, and if that's what you choose to do, I can't stop you. But I do know that once I don't return from where I came within one hour, your beloved sons will be dead. I don't think you killing me would make you feel satisfied knowing that your deliberate actions resulted in your own children being killed. You don't care about me and I don't expect you to, but I do believe you love your children." With his back to me, I was looking in his direction. The moment he turned around again, I looked away.

"I do...love my children; they are all I have ever lived for," he said, solemnly. "We have always stayed together. Their mother died years ago, but I never abandoned them. And I call them *children* just as you humans call your children by that name." He paused for a while. "What do you want? I understand that your family is here. Have you come to ask for their release?"

With those words, I felt like we were finally beginning to get somewhere. I thought for a moment, even though I knew exactly what I was meant to say before I walked in there.

"I will turn my back and you can speak freely," he said. "We will avoid eye contact and it is my gesture of good will in this meeting."

"Okay…" I replied. "I do want my family back…"

"All right. Well then, it's done."

"You don't understand," I continued. "I want my family back, but I want our lives back too. There's not much of a life they can have as zombies—people who can't seem to think or feel, express themselves or show emotions. I want everyone in this place to return home and to continue living their lives with their loved ones. That's what I want and that's what you've taken away from us!"

He shifted his head a little. "You mention the word *love*, Mr. Spader. What do your kind know about love?"

"Everything that matters," I retorted. "The human race is not a perfect race, and despite all the wrong we do and have done, so many of us have done so much good and have shown so much love not just for our own, but for others too. We've shown love for all animals, including your kind. How can you ever deny that?"

"If that were true, you and I wouldn't be here today in this very room and my kind would not have taken over your town. The opposite is true. Many of you have been unkind to animals, especially to the ones you call *man's best friend.* Many of us have been abused, neglected and even put down without a human so-called loved one being there for us in our final hour. They turned their backs on the dogs who had loved them unconditionally for years and years. Your kind has polluted the world with hatred stemming from jealousy, envy, wanting what you ought not to have and taking what you know isn't rightfully yours. Useless wars have erupted and lives lost because you wanted to control one another, enslave one another, dominate one another. And that's why we're here. That is why the forces within the skies have visited this particular town to make the changes that are necessary to save those that remain."

I scoffed at what he said. "You talk about all the bad things we've done—wars, enslavement and all that stuff, but you have a military set up here; you have people enslaved under your nose and you think you're better than we are? You have a huge pit being dug outside where you intend to toss the people you exterminate. You, sir, are no better than the worst humans that ever lived because you cannot justify doing the same evil things they've done simply to get the result you want." I shifted in my seat as the passion in my heart was overwhelming. "Release these people and leave our town! Go back to wherever you came from. Whatever needs fixing in Eppington will be fixed by the people who live here. Tell whomever sent you that we don't need them. Destroy the invisible boundary and put this place back on the map!"

"I see you were well informed," he replied. "And I understand it was one of us who made you privy to that information."

I didn't like the tone of his voice and feared for Hugo's safety. "Hugo is different from you all," I said. "He knows what it is to be grateful to the one who took care of him and to love enough to risk his own life. Maybe you can learn something from him."

"I'm turning around now," he said. "You may look away if you prefer, but just so you know, I have no intention of hypnotizing you in any way."

I appreciated that bit of enlightenment, but stuck with the plan.

He walked back over to his desk and sat down. "I am from another place, as you might have figured out. There are forces in the universe that work for the good of canines and as members of that celestial community, our mission is to pay a visit to every town in every part of the world where our kind has been grossly mistreated, abused and so forth. This is a special mission of ours and your town is the third assignment. However, I have never before come across anyone—any human especially in his youth who would risk his life the way you've done for the sake of the one thing we fight for which is love. I cannot deny the fact that you are here advocating not just for your family—but for every member of this town. I have never witnessed such passion and love in a child so young." He looked away for a moment and seemed genuinely moved. "In light of this fact, I am inclined to consider that perhaps this isn't where we need to be. There are other places that I am sure about, but this is no longer one of them. I have something to seriously consider."

I nodded, but was jumping for joy inside. Was this canine going to bend?

He picked up his cell, dialed a number, then placed it on speakerphone. "Where is Hugo and his human?" he asked.

"They're here," the male voice replied. "Right outside the door."

"Send them in and take Mr. Spader to have a seat out front for a few minutes."

He looked at me, but of course, I avoided eye contact. I didn't trust him that much.

"Please, Mr. Spader, allow me a few minutes to speak with your friends. I will not be long."

I got up just as the door opened and after walking out, Hugo and Jeffreys went inside and shut the door behind them. We'd only glanced at each other in passing. The guard who'd accompanied us to the office, led me over to a nearby chair where I waited.

While there, I reflected on what transpired between the giant of a dog and myself. I could barely believe that I actually pulled this thing off and that Hugo was right on the money when he thought of kidnapping the leader's only family. I imagined what it would be like hugging my folks again and teasing Carl. I missed those things I never thought I'd lose. It's really true that you don't miss the water 'til the well runs dry. I yearned for the expression on my folks' faces when they've woken up out of that terrible nightmare—*any* expression would do. Sitting there, everything that transpired felt surreal. If this dog wasn't lying to me and was considering releasing his grip on this town, our lives would be normal again. Maybe as a result of this experience, we'd do better from now on as a community and would treat the animals with more love and respect. Besides, they deserved it just as much as we did.

I got summoned back to Leader's office a few minutes later. Jeffreys and Hugo walked out before I arrived and I was alone with the mastiff again. He was still at his desk.

"I have made a decision," he started. "I agree to release everyone and to give you your town back and I and others from afar will leave. But you must agree to work on the areas of animal cruelty and neglect that must be addressed. I will give you time as a community, but there must be marked improvement in the way you treat animals in Eppington. If you, as humans, fail in this regard a second time around, we will come back and resume where we'd left off and there will be nothing anyone can do to reverse the decision we have made. Am I clear, Mr. Spader?

"Yes, you are." I readily agreed, and I believe I did so with a smile. I was elated, unlike you could ever imagine, and struggled to keep my composure.

"While you were out front, I contacted my agents and they have agreed with my proposals," he continued. "They will be here at four o'clock promptly. That's three hours from now."

"Will my family be released now?" I asked.

"They will remain here until shortly before that hour, and you will meet them at home. This place will be abandoned. As for my sons, when the spacecraft arrives, they will be elevated from wherever they are."

From my peripheral vision, I could see that he was studying me.

"I know what you're thinking," he added. "You're thinking that if the spacecraft coming here can easily release my sons, why am I meeting your demands."

"You're right," I said.

"It's because the craft would never return unless we decided to depart for good."

"I see."

"So, Mr. Spader, you've won. After today, I hope I will never have to pay another visit to your beloved town ever again."

"I'll do what I can to make sure you don't," I replied.

11

As Jeffreys, Hugo and I walked back through the main building in the direction of the exit, I was in a much better mood than when we'd first arrived. I happened to pass Sam's folks on the northern side closer to where the leader's office was and probably hadn't noticed them before due to the overwhelming grief I'd felt after seeing my folks. Everyone was pretty much doing a lot of nothing and it was distressing to see them in that state. However, I knew it wouldn't be much longer before they were completely free again and had reclaimed their identity. They'd no longer be like robots and mere shells without a soul.

"It won't be much longer!" I said to my family as I approached their cell once more. Carl was now sitting on the floor facing the western side of the wall. Mom and Dad were exactly where I'd left them. "You all will be home soon. I gave you my word."

They didn't have a reaction, but that was okay. Everything would be back to normal soon.

Jeffreys, Hugo and I were in a celebratory mood after we left the compound. We were dancing, singing and shouting for joy in the car. I, of course, made the most noise, especially since I had the most to gain. My folks were coming back home and this nightmare of a reality was going to be a thing of the past. That was the best day of my life.

I called Sam on her cell, told her to put me on speakerphone and I gave her and Rob the great news. They erupted with joy and I had to caution them to quiet down as we were not clear out of the woods yet. They said the canines were still sleeping, which was good to know.

At my urging, Jeffreys agreed to stop at Fredricka's Diner for ice cream. I told him I was buying cones for everyone. Fredricka's had better flavors and their prices were cheaper than local ice cream parlors.

"I'd take a chocolate," Hugo said. "For years, chocolate wasn't good for us dogs, but it doesn't bother us now. This may be the last chance I get to savor its goodness before everything changes to the way it was before."

"I don't blame you," Jeffreys asserted. "You probably should have a double scoop or triple."

I laughed. "Well, I feel like eating a barrel and probably would if I didn't think I'd be bent over with a serious stomach ache tonight."

We all went inside the diner and I picked out a vanilla for Sam and a butter pecan for Rob, which were their favorite. Jeffreys selected a pistachio nut flavor and Hugo grabbed his chocolate—double scoops.

Hugo held Rob's cone and I held Sam's.

"I can't believe we actually did it!" I said, licking my strawberry ice cream.

"Yes indeed, we did," Hugo replied. "Actually—*you* did. You were the one to convince our leader to reconsider what they were doing."

Jeffreys nodded.

"By the way, you guys didn't say why he called you in."

Jeffreys glanced through the rear-view mirror. "I guess you can say Hugo here got a bit of a scolding for his part in this whole deal, but surprisingly, it wasn't too bad. The leader said Hugo's loyalty for his 'human' as he calls me, to the extent that he released me from the daze regardless of the risk involved, amazed him. Hugo came clean with that part. Told me he felt he owed him that much. After that, he called you back in."

"Oh, okay. All is well that ends well, huh?" I replied. "At least, that's what my grandpa used to say."

"Yip," Hugo chimed in. "All is well that ends well."

After popping in at the distillery and giving the guys a couple of high fives, I suddenly remembered something. I told everyone I'd be right back, went downstairs and hopped on my bike.

As I rode toward my house, I tried to suppress the anger that had risen once again inside of me. There was something I needed to do and after that it would no longer be on my chest.

At the house, I dismounted the bike and leaned it against the side of our front porch. I heard the sound of the TV inside and quickly climbed the steps.

On opening the door, I found Dillinger sitting on the couch with a glass of red wine parked next to him.

"Hewey Spader..." he smiled. "I thought you had moved on permanently."

"You should be so lucky, huh?" I boldly replied, without making eye contact. I wasn't sure of his abilities. So, I wasn't about to take the chance looking him in the eye, especially after the guys and I had come so far.

"So, you're speaking now. It's no longer a big act," he added.

"Guess that means you knew all along..."

"Uh-huh."

"Look, Dillinger, I came here to tell you something."

"I'm all ears." He shifted fully in my direction.

I stood in the middle of the living room. "What you did to us was plain evil," I started.

"Evil?"

"Shut up and let me talk! You are one of probably the few dogs in this neighborhood that got treated like a frigging king. You were loved, fed, given a good shelter and you turned around and betrayed us; had my folks shipped out like they'd been cruel to you. I never imagined in a million years that you wanted anything but the best for all of us, but this experience showed us exactly who you are."

"You're taking things way out of perspective, Hewey."

I shook my head quickly. "I'm not and you know it. You saw an opportunity to take over my folks' house and live a selfish life, and you took it. We loved you, but it was clear, you didn't love us back."

"I loved you enough to know you were out there and I didn't say anything to anyone," he replied. "I didn't give you up."

I sighed. "I'm not sure why you didn't, but that one thing doesn't justify the bad things you've done. I want you out of here today."

"You're giving me orders, Hewey Spader?"

"You're intelligent enough to understand, Dillinger."

"Well, maybe it's time for me to turn you in."

"Do so. See if anyone listens to you." I returned to the door. "Be gone before four o'clock today. If I find you here when I get back, I'll get you out myself."

I slammed the door behind me and left him with something to think about.

Jeffreys and Hugo stayed with us at the distillery until later that afternoon. We had been checking our cell phone clocks almost every minute from 3:40 P.M. onwards. At 4:00, to our amazement and relief, we all witnessed Brick and Dutch, while chained, vanish out of those chairs right in front of our eyes. The mastiff had told the truth.

There was a collective cheer in the room and shortly thereafter, Jeffreys and Hugo decided it was time for them to leave.

Afterwards, I asked the guys, "Do you know what this means?"

"Our folks are home!" Sam exclaimed. "Let's go!"

"Group hug before we split up?" Rob asked.

"Group hug," Sam readily agreed.

We all hugged tightly and shed tears of joy. We'd been through hell and survived.

We got on our bikes and rode together until the time came for us to part ways. Immediately, we saw the difference in our neighborhood. Julio Perez was outside dumping the trash and I could hear Christian music blaring from the Rivera's house. Another neighbor, Joe McAlpine, was giving his Shih-tzu a sudsy bath in a plastic tub."

"Hey, Hewey!" He waved with suds all over his white tee shirt.

"How you doin', Joe?" I waved back. It was so good to hear his voice.

Donna Farnham was outside giggling and playing with her kids, Michael and Sara. The laughter sounded heavenly and I remember smiling while passing by. I'd glanced at Mrs. Christie's house and couldn't help thinking how we'd never see her again and she would no longer be the brunt of some of our jokes. How she'd lost her life in the midst of all that confusion saddened me. Now, that things were obviously back to normal, I was hopeful that her murder would be investigated.

I couldn't wait to get home and when I finally arrived, I believed the wheels were still spinning after I'd hopped off the bike. When I opened the front door, the scene I beheld before me was heavenly. Carl was playing a game on TV and my parents were talking at the dining room table.

When they saw me, they all hurried over in my direction and we hugged so tightly for what felt like hours.

"So, you remember?" I asked them, after we finally loosened our grip.

"Yes, we do," Mom said. "We heard every word you said when we were at that terrible place, son, but for some reason, we couldn't respond."

"You kept your word, didn't you?" Carl smiled.

"He surely did," Dad said.

I could see he was proud of me. They all were and they said so.

"Because of you, honey, everything's back to normal now," Mom remarked. "You have to tell us everything."

"Do you have about three hours?" I asked.

They all laughed.

"Wait a minute! Where's Dillinger?" I noticed he was nowhere in sight.

"We don't know. He wasn't here when we got back," Mom said.

"Cool," I replied.

Two days later…

"Hewey, would you go get the newspaper from the porch?" Mom asked, after I emerged from my room for breakfast. She, Dad and Carl were sitting at the kitchen counter. We preferred to have breakfast there instead of at the table, for some unknown reason.

"Sure, Mom," I said, rubbing my eyes.

It was so good to have slept in my own bed for the past two nights after sleeping on mats for more than a week. I'd heard from the guys and everything was good on their side of the neighborhood. Sam said that her neighbors were all back and everyone acted friendlier. A good change, especially on her street when a good many of those residents were sort of stuck up and couldn't seem to crack a smile towards each other.

I opened the door and met the newspaper balled up right in front of it. It was good to know they were back in production. I picked it up and closed the door, then handed it to Mom.

"Pancakes, huh?" I said, taking a seat next to her.

"Your favorite." She smiled, opening the newspaper.

I wasted no time digging in. Blueberries on top had my mouth watering from the second I spotted them.

"Oh, my gosh!" Mom exclaimed, gazing down at the paper, wide-eyed. Dad leaned in. Carl couldn't care less.

"What's the matter?" I asked as my chewing slowed down.

"Our neighbor, Clyde Rivera, is in police custody. They have his picture here brisk and bold!"

"Why was he arrested?" I grimaced.

"It says here that he confessed to his wife last evening that he killed Johnette Christie! Suzanne turned him in."

"What? How can that be?" *Shocked* wasn't the word for me.

"He admitted to have been having a secret affair with Johnette behind Suzanne's back and said Johnette threatened to tell Suzanne about the affair after he told her he was going to end it. He said he knew it was wrong and felt guilty about it."

"So, Mrs. Christie was seeing three guys?" I blurted.

Mom and Dad looked my way. "What are you talking about, Hewey?" Mom asked.

That was my cue to shut up. They had no idea that the guys and I had been spying on Mrs. Christie for a long time. The fact that she was seeing two men behind her husband's back shocked me, mainly because we had no inkling about the other guy. I wondered what time he used to make it over to her place.

"But he killed Mrs. Christie while everyone were basically zombies around here," I said to them. "It makes me wonder if somehow he avoided drinking the same *crazy juice* all the rest of you had. And instead, was in his right mind like me and the guys were. It might explain how he could've gotten angry enough to kill her. I doubt he would've been able to if he was under that *spell*."

Dad was nodding his head. "You may have a point, son, but on the other hand, I'm sure police officers still had the ability to shoot people if they felt the need to. So, we can't dismiss the possibility that Clyde did that while dazed."

"I guess we won't know unless someone asks him, huh?" Carl chimed in.

"Maybe someday I will, but right now, I'm not that interested. I've gotta take a shower and get dressed. None of us has seen Jase or his mother since everyone returned home."

"Really?" Mom asked. "I hope they're all right."

"Me too," I said. I took up my last bite and got up from the counter.

After I had a quick shower and got dressed, I met Sam and Rob outside sitting on the porch.

"Ready, guys?" I asked, shutting the front door.

"Ready like Freddy," Rob replied.

As we were about to hop onto our bikes, Jeffreys was walking Hugo on a leash.

"A wonderful morning to you guys." Jeffreys waved.

"Morning!" We all said, hurrying over to them. I started petting Hugo who was no longer walking on hind legs or talking, but was back to being a regular dog.

Sam caressed Hugo's head. "Good to see ya, big guy. Jeffreys treating you well?" She glanced at Jeffreys with a smile.

It didn't appear that he approved of her question. "I think the answer to that will forever lie in the way we both interacted as of late. Don't you think so, young lady?"

"Yeah. You're definitely right." Her smile slowly disappeared.

"So, where are you guys headed?" he asked.

"We're going over to Jase's house again," I said. "He and his mom haven't been seen since they were at the compound."

"That's strange." Jeffreys frowned. "I hope they turn up soon."

And that was twenty-five years ago. No one has seen Jase or his mother ever since. We'd all come out of the *curse of Eppington*, as I think is now fitting to call it, but I'm not sure that Jase and his mom ever did. It's a mystery to this day.

~ End of Book Two ~

KEEP READING FOR BOOK THREE
– Let Sleeping Dogs Lie…

*** Living in different parts of the world, the guys have a reunion more than two decades after the strange events that took place in their hometown of Eppington. They meet to discuss the possibility of getting to the bottom of what happened to their friend Jase and his mother. Will they uncover the shocking truth? Find out in book three of this thrilling series. ***

HEWEY SPADER COZY MYSTERY SERIES
BOOK THREE

LET SLEEPING DOGS LIE

#1 BEST SELLING AUTHOR
TANYA R. TAYLOR

LET SLEEPING DOGS LIE

HEWEY SPADER COZY MYSTERY SERIES
BOOK THREE

Thank you, Oswaldo, Christian and Mercedes, for making my world bright and for being my inspiration. You are deeply loved. xxx

1

I wasn't sure how to feel after my long distance call with Rob ended. It was the first time we'd spoken since we'd grown up and pretty much went our separate ways. Our hometown of Eppington had been left far behind since the three of us—Rob, Sam, and I—had escaped to college, each starting over in a new city, and in Sam's case, a new country. Rob and I had communicated regularly, but soon, the phone calls became less and less frequent. On the other hand, Sam and I had kept in touch for the longest time until shortly after she'd met a guy in college whom she referred to as her *soulmate*. Not wanting to crowd her, I eventually decided it was best to just give her her space.

When we were teenagers, I'd secretly hoped that someday Sam would think of me as more than a best friend. Goodness knows I loved the girl to the moon and back, and worshipped the ground she walked on. Never mind the fact that she wasn't a *girly girl* and she dressed like a tomboy. As far as I was concerned, she was all woman and everything I needed in my life.

But I never got around to telling her that.

Deep inside, I wondered if she'd ever once considered giving me the time of day. Forget about all the mischievous things she, Rob, Jase and I did as kids and the times we hung out together on the top floor of the distillery after school spying on our neighbors, especially Mrs. Johnette Christie, who was later murdered during that *questionable period* in our lives. And who could forget Mr. and Mrs. Rivera a couple of doors down; not to mention the old grouch, Julio

Perez, who lived next door to the saintly couple. Mr. Clyde Rivera, once a God-fearing man had been jailed for murdering Mrs. Christie, also during that *questionable period*. As it turns out, they were secret lovers.

The guys and I had spent countless hours on Lake Olivia fishing which was our favorite pastime. Considering the amount of time Sam and I had spent together, though largely in the company of Rob and Jase, you'd think she would've viewed *me* as her soulmate instead of some strange guy she'd meet years later in college. No one else on the planet understood the girl better than I did and that should've counted for something. But I guess it didn't.

So, what's a young man to do other than to cut his losses and move on to the next cutie pie willing to give him the time of day? And that's exactly what I did.

After finishing college with a computer engineering degree—an accomplishment my folks were immensely proud of since I'd been a goof-off for most of my high school years—I remained in New Mexico and worked for a large software company. I'd put in eighteen years there and loved every minute of it. However, after raking in enough cash to pay off my condo and leaving a healthy chunk of it in the bank, I decided to start my own business. All of a sudden, I was the one doing the hiring and earning much more on my own than I'd ever thought possible.

Sam had become a hotshot attorney in France, and Rob, who'd fallen in love with sunny Florida, opened up a couple of bistros there in Orlando.

Decades had passed since any of us had set eyes on each other and that phone call I'd made to Rob that cloudy day in July was the catalyst that would bring the three of us full circle. After graduating high school, we'd never uttered a single word to one another regarding our experience many years ago in our hometown of Eppington until that day I'd spoken with Rob. I realized that he, too, never truly found peace of mind, knowing our best friend, Jase, and his mother had disappeared without a trace.

I left the task up to Rob to contact Sam since he'd actually seen her a year earlier when she was in Orlando with her husband to take care of some business. She and Rob had exchanged phone numbers then, though none had bothered to contact each other ever since. Rob had told me he didn't get a good vibe from the husband who was at least a foot taller than he was and looked like a bodybuilder. Maybe it was a jealousy thing on the husband's part and Rob was wondering if Sam should've offered to give him her number in the first place. In any event, I left it to him to get in touch with her as I certainly didn't want to stir up anything between Sam and her supposed *soulmate*. Rob admitted they'd only spoken for a few minutes, reminiscing on old times. Jase's name came up, but as the mood subsequently changed, they parted ways with a great big hug and the promise of "catching up".

It was a few days later when I got a call from Rob saying that Sam agreed for us to meet in Eppington three weeks later. My folks' house would be the venue. We had one mission in mind and it was to get to the bottom of what happened to Jase and his mom once and for all.

2

I can't describe how nervous I was knowing I was about to see Sam again after being apart for so long. As I quietly sat in the plane contemplating our reunion with my head leaning against the head rest, I wasn't sure what I was going to do when we met. Would I hug her or just say *hello*? It was bound to be an awkward moment; in fact, I was convinced of it. I'd never forgotten her radiant smile or the sound of her voice. There was no way I possibly could. Truth be told—if I'd thought about her once since the last day I'd seen her, I'd thought about her a million times. What was so strange was I didn't remember having such strong feelings towards her when we were kids, compared to when we'd all moved away. Maybe it was that *not missing the water 'til the well runs dry* sort of deal. I really think that's it. Anyway, the day of reckoning was here. I tried to clear my head of all the distracting thoughts and to keep focused on the mission at hand which was the most important thing.

"Are you all right, deary?" The lovely old lady sitting next to me asked.

She had a heavenly glow about her narrow, little face and a demeanor like that of my sweet grandma who'd passed away when I was nine. She was short and thin—with shoulder-length gray hair.

"I'm fine, thanks," I answered with a slight smile.

"I only asked, son, because you seem to have a lot on your mind."

"It's that obvious?" I arched my brows, moving my head away from the head rest.

"I'm afraid so," she replied. "I always make it a point to ask if someone is all right whenever the thought crosses my mind because these days, so many people are keeping dreadful things to themselves that they have no business carrying alone. We can all use a listening ear or helping hand from time to time. Don't you agree?"

"To be honest, I'm going home to see a couple of friends I hadn't seen in ages," I told her. "A bit nervous about it, that's all."

"Oh, I see! Well, if that's all it is, that's quite all right then." She quickly patted my knee. "If it's any consolation, just reminisce on all the good times you all have shared and gradually, you should feel that nervousness going away. Works for me every time."

I nodded, appreciatively. "That's great advice, ma'am. Thank you."

"Glad to have been of help."

I retreated to my former position; this time shutting my eyes. The old lady's humble suggestion was one I'd decided to take. As pleasant scenes of when the guys and I were kids sailed through my mind, it wasn't long before I drifted right off to sleep.

* * * *

It seemed like hours had passed before I'd heard the woman's voice again.

"Sonny, you'd better wake up now!"

I felt a feeble shake of my arm.

"Huh?" I opened my eyes, trying to remember exactly where I was.

"The pilot just said that we'll be arriving shortly, so I didn't want you to get left behind in this plane," she said.

Getting myself together, I laughed at the idea, though rather weakly. "Thanks. I appreciate it."

"You're very welcome, deary."

Our descent at the Eppington International Airport was as smooth as could be, and thankfully, the entire flight from New Mexico was largely uneventful. I felt a bit tired and looked forward to grabbing a hot cup of cappuccino from the airport's deli.

I checked my wristwatch the moment the plane landed. It was 10:35 A.M.

"Well, we're here," the old lady said. "Thankfully, we've all arrived in one piece."

"Yeah." I agreed.

As the hatch opened and she, along with others stood to gather their items, I remained seated by the window.

Slowly, dozens of passengers trailed past our row toward the exit.

"Aren't you coming?" the lady asked with her purse in hand or do you want them to fly you right back to New Mexico?"

I chuckled. "I'd rather wait for everyone else to leave first."

"My! That's really generous of you! Well, it was nice meeting you."

"It was nice meeting you too."

"I'm Trudy, by the way. Surname's Balfour." She extended her hand.

"Hewey Spader." I returned the handshake.

She stepped out into the aisle and gradually trailed along with the others ahead of her. I gathered she wasn't an Eppington native because I would've recognized the accent.

As the last four persons were leaving the aircraft, I got up and reached overhead for my luggage. A lovely stewardess kindly shut the compartment for me after I'd grabbed the bags.

"Thanks so much," I told her.

"My pleasure." She smiled. "Thanks for flying with us."

The first thing I did was made my way to the nearest deli and grabbed that cappuccino I desperately wanted. I prefer cappuccino over regular coffee as it tends to give me that boost I often need throughout the day.

Outside, I caught a waiting cab and within a half an hour of landing, I was on my way to my parent's house.

3

Three years had passed since I'd flown back home for a visit. The last time I was there was to attend our parents' funeral after they'd both been killed in an horrific car accident. I'd kept in touch with my brother, Carl, but avoided our house because I knew it would bring back so many memories I just wasn't ready to deal with. Losing two parents at the same time was a heavy blow for both of us. I realized to some degree it was selfish of me to have not returned sooner, knowing that Carl had to face the reality of their loss every day since he'd never bothered to move out of the house. But I'd convinced myself that I had to be in touch with my feelings, aware of what I could handle and allow myself time to grieve in my own way in order to protect my sanity.

Our folks meant everything to Carl and me. We used to be a tight-knit family and every year after I'd moved away, I either came back to see them or paid for a vacation for all of us to meet up somewhere else. My family was all I had despite the distance between us, and when Mom and Dad died, I felt I'd lost a huge part of my identity. Suddenly, I no longer had folks and even as a grown man, I can't begin to express how that reality truly affected me.

After entering my subdivision, the closer we got to the house, the more unsure I was of my feelings about being there. I knew I had to be strong because I hated the feeling of being out of control.

Carl was outside working on his red motorbike when my cab pulled up in front of the house. He was wearing some faded jeans and a white spotted tee shirt. Despite his scruffy appearance, he still had that baby face which made him look like he'd barely aged since we were teenagers.

Carl was a mechanic by trade, as evident by the vehicles he had on jack stands in front of our folks' house. Mom used to give him a hard time for having a lot of cars in the yard at once, especially the ones that looked like they belonged in the junk yard instead. She said harboring vehicles like that for extended periods brought down the quality of the neighborhood. Carl did manage to upkeep the house though—fresh paint every year, clean windows and a well-manicured lawn. He had pride in his surroundings which spilled over into his work. He was one of the best mechanics in town and as quickly as he managed to clear up cars from in front of our house, others would be brought there for service or repair.

Fortunately, he was permitted to operate his small mechanic business in our neighborhood since none of the neighbors complained, and he hadn't any signage. Saved him overhead expenses, for sure.

I reached over and paid the cab driver, got out of the vehicle and grabbed my luggage from the popped trunk. Carl looked at me, stood up and shoved his hands into his pockets. His expression was blank; much different than I was used to.

As the cab drove away, I walked towards him. "Hey, li'l brother! How are you doing?"

"Okay," he replied, as I got within a few feet of him.

I dropped the luggage and gave him a big hug, but I could feel the coldness.

"What's the matter?" I asked. "You don't look that thrilled to see me."

He wiped off his hands with the old rag he was holding. "Good to see you. How long will you be here?" He led the way to the front door.

"A couple of weeks at least."

"Okay. Well…your room is pretty much the way you left it when you were here three years ago." He walked inside and held the door the open for me. "And you can probably remember where everything else is."

"Yeah." I set the luggage down again and looked at him as we stood awkwardly together in the living room.

"Anyway, I'm gonna get cleaned up, then I'll be going out for a while," he added, before starting down the hallway.

"Carl…"

"Yeah?" He turned around.

"What's up with you? You don't seem like yourself."

"Me?" He took a few steps forward. "You're the one who's changed, Hewey. You went away, became a big shot and only looked back at us once or twice a year whenever you were good and ready. I was here with Mom and Dad, taking care of everything they needed while you lived the good life."

"That's a damn lie and you know it, Carl! I never turned my back on any of you. Mom and Dad needed for nothing because I made sure they didn't. How could you say such a thing?"

"You think just because you showed up here, you deserve some special privilege, huh? I'm not Mom and Dad, Hewey. I don't kiss up to anybody. He sucked his teeth. "I'm not getting into this. I'm gonna take a shower."

He continued down the hallway toward the bathroom.

I shook my head and sauntered over to the window at the southern side of the living room. Looking outside, I recalled the countless times Carl and I had rolled our bicycles on that side of the house from the backyard where they were often kept. He was annoying even back then, but we got along. I wasn't sure what had happened.

Turning to my right towards where the kitchen stood, I envisioned Mom there making breakfast while Dad sat at the counter reading the newspaper. That was pretty much their early morning routine and I remember being so happy and feeling secure as a kid just having them as my folks. Then there were pictures of all of us on the walls; some were of Mom and Dad only and others of us as a family. Within minutes, the emotions I thought I'd conquered overwhelmed me as the memories came flooding back. I sat on the sofa, covered my face and just wept. Everywhere reminded me of my folks and in my mind, I could even hear their voices still. It's the very reason I'd stayed away for so long. I wanted more than anything to avoid those feelings and now I was thinking that maybe I'd returned too soon.

After a good cry, I got up and went into my parents' room, but only stood at the door. The first place my eyes landed were on their king-sized bed. It was neatly draped with Mom's favorite bedspread and her dresser still had all her favorite perfumes on top. Dad's brown robe was hanging on the standing rack near his bureau and I could see him wearing it as he walked about the house. More tears fell, but by then, I knew I'd already gotten out a lot of what I had bottled up inside for so long.

"I love you both," I whispered, before leaving the room.

Carl exited the bathroom with a towel tied around his waist, then headed into his room.

I went to my bedroom and sat on the bed. Carl was right—everything was basically the way I'd left it three years ago after the funeral. I didn't remember it being as clean though, but I'm sure I had him to thank for it.

I stretched out on my back and folded my arms behind my head.

A few minutes later, Carl appeared in my doorway dressed in a dark blue jeans and a yellow cotton shirt. He'd obviously had a shave.

"You asleep?" he asked.

"No," I answered, sitting up.

"I'm heading out now. Got an early lunch date with Tamara. You remember her, don't you?"

"You mean Tamara Hinsley—Mom's best friend's daughter?"

"Yeah—her. She was at the funeral…"

"Yeah, I know. She's a nice girl. Always had her eyes on you since you were sixteen."

"Sure…right." He managed a slight smile. "So, what're you up to?"

I rubbed my chin. "Rob and Samantha are in town and they're coming over for a while."

"Yeah. You said on the phone you guys had some catching up to do."

I was beginning to wonder if this was the same guy who'd treated me so coldly when I arrived. I figured his conscience had gotten to him.

"Anyway, I'm off. A spare of keys for the house are on the kitchen counter."

"Thanks, bro."

After Carl pulled off in his jeep, I carried my luggage into my bedroom and pulled out the chardonnay I'd brought with me from New Mexico. I figured our first meeting in decades should be one celebrated with a quality white wine and good conversation before we embarked on the mission at hand.

Immediately, I placed the wine in the freezer so that it would be chilled by the time the guys got here.

4

I nervously checked my watch several times before Sam and Rob were due to arrive. The time we'd settled on was one o'clock.

I paced back and forth through the living room, then went on the back porch at one point and caught a smoke. I'd quit smoking a year earlier, but couldn't resist a pack of Marlboro's while grabbing my coffee at the airport. Mom would've been disappointed if she knew I'd relapsed, if only once. She never understood how I'd managed to pick up such a bad habit and had warned me over and repeatedly that I could be looking at a future with lung cancer if I didn't quit. After a few years of enduring her stern rebuke, I finally decided to take heed and I quit cold turkey.

Needless to say how proud she was of me. Yet, here I am now—trying to smoke away my anxiety over meeting with a girl I'd known practically all of my childhood. I shook my head in disgust, tossed the cigarette to the ground and squashed it with my shoe. I resented the idea that a grown man like me could be so shamefully weak. Sam was like one of the guys and that's how I needed to remember her.

I heard a vehicle pull up. It was definitely one of them. I sprang up, hurried inside and closed the door behind me, then rushed over to the front room window to get a peak outside. Sam and Rob were exiting a black Camry and suddenly, at the sight of Sam, my knees felt weak. I realized I was behaving like a punk again, but there was nothing I do to stop the nervousness that had cruelly resurfaced. I hurried over to the rectangular mirror attached to the wall at the front of the hallway, ensuring I still looked presentable in my light brown trousers and white dress shirt I was wearing. I straightened my collar and did a final pat of my slicked back hair and figured right then and there it was now or never.

The doorbell rang, and convincing myself to *man up*, I coolly walked over and opened the door.

"Hewey!" Rob exclaimed on the other side. Sam was standing behind him.

"My man!" I said, as we immediately locked into a bear hug.

"It's been ages!" he said. "Before you called, I was beginning to wonder if we'd ever see one another again."

"I was beginning to wonder the same thing."

Smiling, Sam stepped forward. "Hey, Hewey."

Rob stepped aside.

"Sam…it's really good to see you," I told her, mesmerized by how beautiful she was. She was always breathtaking, but adulthood had been even kinder to her. She almost looked like a different person, especially since she was actually wearing a dress that day. It was literally the first time I'd ever seen Sam in a dress, not to mention the makeup which enhanced her natural beauty.

"Don't I get a hug?" she asked. "Rob here got his. What am I—*chopped liver*?"

I stepped outside and gave her a warm hug, remembering that she was a lady—now, more than ever—and I didn't want to let her go.

Rob cleared his throat. "I think it's been like five minutes you two have been locked in this position. My bear hug wasn't even a good ten seconds."

Sam and I chuckled as we gently parted ways.

"When did you guys arrive in town?" I asked.

"I flew in yesterday," Rob indicated. "Sam got here a couple of hours ago."

"I just landed after ten," I said. "Oh! Don't know what I was thinking…please come inside, guys."

"Bro, it's been decades!" Rob exclaimed, having a seat on the sofa.

Sam sat on the couch where I joined her while leaving ample space between us, of course.

"Yeah. Twenty-five years to be exact," I replied.

"Has it really been that long?" Sam asked.

"Yep." I nodded. "Time surely flies. After we graduated high school in '98, we all went to college and that was it."

"Strange how that happened for the three of us, huh?" Sam crossed her legs. Her black, sleeveless dress stopped a couple of inches above her knees revealing her flawless skin, while her red painted toenails poked through the open front tip of her black shoes.

"I guess we all just wanted to get the hell outta this town, especially after what we'd been through," Rob remarked.

"Certainly was true for me," Sam noted. "I dreaded the thought that what happened before could possibly happen again. Even tried to convince my peeps that we should all just pack up and move to another city, if not another country altogether. But Mom and Dad thought what happened here in Eppington could happen anywhere else and there was no sense in running. Rob's peeps obviously saw things differently since they got out of here, eventually."

"Surely did." Rob agreed. "When I went away to college, they moved to Dallas. Been there ever since."

"I see you moved to a whole other country," I said to Sam.

She sighed. "To be honest, every day I spent here since that spacecraft appeared and even throughout my college years, I was fearful. I couldn't imagine having to live through another nightmare like that, so as quick as I could get through law school, I went as far away from this country as I could. Figured France was far enough. I took some extra courses while there and passed the French bar exam, and it wasn't long before I landed a good job working for a major company in their legal department."

"So, you weren't practicing—like in a courtroom?" I asked.

She shook her head. "No and that's fine with me. I figured if I ever started my own practice, that's when the courtroom drama'll come in."

"And we know drama's right up your alley!" Rob said.

"Very funny." Sam smiled. "By the way…where's Carl, Hewey?"

"Out on a lunch date," I replied.

"Ooh!" She winked. "Have you met her yet?"

"She's actually a friend of the family."

"I see."

"So, how are you guys' folks doing?" I asked both of them.

"My folks are chilling, man," Rob replied. "Said leaving this town was the best decision they ever made."

"Good to know they're happy where they are," I said.

"Mom and Dad are doing okay," Sam answered. "Retired now and enjoying every minute of it, even though Mom says having Dad around her twenty-four-seven drives her nuts sometimes."

I grinned. "Imagine that! What about your sister, Taylor? What's she up to these days?"

"She works as an editor in New York and just got engaged. He's a wonderful guy; worships the ground she walks on. The wedding's set for next year June."

"Wow! That's great." I smiled.

She then leaned forward, holding her wine glass above her knees. "Hewey, I'm really sorry about what happened to your Mom and Dad. I meant to call you, but…"

"It's okay. Believe me," I quickly interjected.

"No, it's not. I didn't have your phone number at the time, but I could've found out what it was. I just thought that maybe I'd be intruding in your life after we hadn't been in touch for so long."

"I understand," I replied, although I really didn't. I couldn't fathom what would make her think she'd be intruding in my life.

"It was quite a shock when I did find out," Rob added. "If I'd known earlier, I would've flown down for the funeral."

"It's really okay, guys. We'd lost touch, so I didn't expect any of you to be there. I know if things were different…"

"Yes, if things were different, we would've been a real support to you at a time like that and I'm sorry we weren't here for you," Sam expressed.

"I know." I cleared my throat. "Now, if you guys don't mind, how about we leave all of that in the past?"

She and Rob glanced at each other. They must've figured right then that it was a topic I wasn't really comfortable discussing.

"I have some chardonnay chilling in the freezer. Can I offer you guys a drink? If not, I'm gonna have one anyway."

"Sure. I'd love one," Sam replied.

"Need you ask?" Rob looked at me incredulously.

I went to the kitchen, retrieved three wine glasses from the cabinet and poured out the chardonnay. I'd located Mom's tray in the exact spot she'd always kept it and rested the glasses on top.

"Here you are." I returned to the living room, allowing Sam and Rob to each grab a glass.

After placing the tray on the center table, I sat down with mine.

"Hmm…this is good." Sam uttered, after having a sip.

"Came all the way from France right to my front door in New Mexico," I revealed.

"You ordered it online?" she asked, curiously.

"Yep."

"Expensive taste."

"With all that money Hewey makes in that software company of his, he can easily afford it," Rob commented.

"You're talking about me, *Mr. Bistro owner with multiple locations*?" I said.

Sam grinned. "We all did pretty well for ourselves, didn't we?"

I leaned back comfortably on the couch. "We surely did, despite everything."

Rob was nodding. "My mom wanted me to be an engineer like you, but you know how much I love food—opening a bistro was the only way to go."

Sam and I had a good chuckle. Rob had clearly packed on at least an extra thirty pounds since we were kids and considering the industry he was in and how much he liked to eat, the fact that he'd gained so much weight was no surprise to me. He still wore his extra poundage pretty well though.

The guys and I spent the greater part of an hour reminiscing about old times and how much fun we had being mischievous. Jase's name came up a few times in jest and soon I noticed the atmosphere of our conversing had gradually changed from cheerful to slightly dismal.

"I guess we'd better get to the reason we're all here today," I finally said.

"Yeah." Sam agreed.

"Any of you seen Jeffreys since we left?" Rob asked.

"I haven't," Sam replied. "Honestly, I rarely came home for visits, and when I did, I was never here that long."

"I saw Jeffreys a couple of years before my folks…" I paused, not wanting to bring the *accident thing* up again. "I went to his house to see how he was doing, but he was so different—merely a shell of the man he'd been before Hugo died."

"He must've taken Hugo's death so hard," Rob said.

"Yeah. That dog was his only family and best friend in the world," I returned.

Sam was quiet; obviously contemplating Jeffreys' loss.

"We spoke for a while, but just random stuff. I got the sense he didn't get many visitors and probably wasn't keen on it anyway."

"He never was very sociable to begin with," Sam noted. "So, it made sense that he'd isolate himself even more after losing Hugo. Poor guy."

I rested my half-empty glass of chardonnay on the center table. "I think speaking with Jeffreys, just for us to put our heads together to get a recap of what happened when everyone else was being held captive, would be a good starting point for us. What do you guys think?"

"I agree," Sam said. "Then we can check in with some of the other neighbors around here who were confined along with Jase and his mom."

"Chief Mays too," I suggested.

"Good idea." Rob nodded. "It's been twenty-five years. That's way too long for us not knowing what happened to our best friend and his mom. Someone has to do something about it and it has to be us."

"You're right," Sam replied. "I'd like to think if the same thing happened to me and one of my peeps that you guys would do whatever you could to find out what happened."

"That's what friends are for." I picked up my wine again.

We decided to use the rest of the day to get settled and to embark on our quest the following day after breakfast.

5

The next day...

"Why in the world are you staying at a hotel, Rob?" Sam asked as Rob chauffeured us in his rented Camry. "I knew you guys sold your house a long time ago, but you could've stayed with me and my peeps."

"Because I'm a tourist, that's why," he answered. "Don't I look like one with this big straw hat I'm wearing?"

"You look like *something*, bro," I remarked. "Not sure what that is yet."

Sam chuckled.

"Rob knew he could've stayed with me too, but he refused." I told her.

"Like I said...I'm a tourist whenever I come here and I like to *feel* like one. Staying with either of you guys would be like I'm a native when being a native here's a thing of the past for me," Rob explained.

"You'll always be a native, Rob." Sam shook her head. "I see you're still the same old you."

Watching them from the back seat reminded me of all the times those two got into it when we were teenagers.

"Same old me for sure," Rob responded, quite happily. "What…?" He glanced her way. "You were hoping adulthood would change me?"

"Not for a second." She sighed. "I love the annoying little dimwit you've always been.

"And I love you too." He leaned over to her; his shoulder meeting hers.

She shoved him slightly. "Focus on the road, big boy."

Rob had grown up physically, but he still had a playful side to him. While Sam, Jase and I had a more serious demeanor, he balanced us off perfectly.

"Now that our bellies are full, we can go and check on Jeffreys," he said.

"Right on!" Sam exclaimed.

"I still think we should've paid Jeffreys a visit first, instead of leaving the neighborhood, coming back, then having to go right back again to find Chief Mays," I said. "Seems pretty backwards to me."

"I'd have to agree with Rob on this one," Sam replied. "I, personally, don't do well trying to start my day without first having a nice breakfast and a huge cup of coffee. And by us going to the diner early this morning, it would've given Jeffreys more time to wake up and get himself together too. No sense landing on the man's doorstep when he might not have had time to at least get his own breakfast and whatever else he needed to get done early. Some folks are crotchety when they wake up in the morning and I have a feeling Jeffreys' one of 'em." She glanced at her wristwatch. "It's now ten past ten. Good time to show up at anybody's house."

"I guess you're right," I replied, although I was accustomed to getting up at five-thirty, grabbing a cup of coffee, then diving straight into my work, which had been my daily routine for the past two decades. Breakfast was often taken care of around mid-morning, and lunch, later in the afternoon. Dinner wasn't a consistent thing for me which means I only ate in the evenings if I was hungry. But I found downing multiple cups of coffee throughout the day significantly decreased my appetite.

As for Jeffreys, I wondered how he was going to react when he saw the three of us again. It was bound to be a real surprise.

"I wanna ask you two a question," Sam started.

"Shoot!" Rob blurted.

"Why are you guys still single? You're in your forties now."

"You go first, Rob," I said.

He glanced at me through the rearview mirror. "Slickster!'

I just shook my head.

"I almost got married once," he told Sam.

"What do you mean...*almost*?" She frowned.

"I'd hired a really sexy Puerto Rican gal to work at one of my bistros. She was perfect in every way you can imagine."

"So, what happened?" Sam probed.

"Turns out she was really a man."

I burst out laughing.

"I had no idea," he continued.

Sam was clearly shocked. "How in the world did you find out?"

Rob suddenly didn't look so cheery anymore; as a matter of fact, he seemed a little embarrassed. "Well, after we'd gotten engaged, more specifically, a couple of months before our big wedding day was to arrive, I tried convincing her that we ought to test the waters to see if we're really compatible…if you know what I mean."

"Uh-huh." Sam waited, and so did I with tears of laughter in my eyes.

"That's when she confessed—that she was born a man. Mind you, she had the surgery and all, but I couldn't deal with it. Just wasn't my cup of tea."

He glanced back at me again. "Would you stop laughing, Hewey! It's not funny."

"The hell it ain't!" I laughed even louder.

By that time, Sam was obviously trying her best not to show him she'd found the story just as amusing as I did.

"So, what happened after that?" she asked him, her voice breaking.

He gulped. "I asked her why she didn't tell me sooner, but she said she was scared and would've done so eventually before we actually tied the knot. I was devastated; just devastated. I broke off the engagement; told her I wasn't gonna fire her because I knew she needed the job, but she ended up leaving the bistro a few days later and deep inside, I was glad she did. It was an awkward few days since she dropped that bomb on me."

"Good thing you asked her about testing the waters first," Sam replied with that subtle grin on her face, which quickly turned into a bigger grin, then she burst out laughing too.

"I can't believe you guys are killing yourself laughing at me!" Rob retorted. "Where's the compassion? That was a really tough time for me, you know?"

"I'm sorry, Rob." Sam again tried to control herself, but was failing miserably.

"Yeah, me too." I managed to blurt the words out.

"You guys are sickening." He shook his head. "My two best friends in the world are having a field day over my former plight."

Soon, Sam was able to collect herself. "I'm sorry for laughing, Rob; I really shouldn't have," she said. "It just sounded so funny, that's all."

"Mind you, if she chose to live her life as a woman after being born a man, that was totally her choice," Rob noted. "My preference is a woman who was born a woman—and what made it even worse was that she deceived me. We were dating for nearly a year and she never came clean with me until after we were engaged. How could I trust a person like that?"

"I see what you mean." I was drying my face with the back of my hand. "Anyway, buddy..." I patted his shoulder, "...there are more fish in the sea."

"You're right." He nodded.

"Now, it's your turn," Sam told me. "Did you have a similar experience?"

"No! No!" I quickly said. "The truth of the matter is, I just never found *Miss Right*. She seemed elusive all this time and I wasn't about to marry just anybody just for marrying sake."

"Seems wise," she replied.

A few moments went by, then I reluctantly said, "So, since you're the only hitched one in the crew, what can we look forward to when it comes to married life?"

She sighed. "Well, it's certainly different from being single."

"Obviously…but what do you mean by that?" Rob asked her.

"Suddenly, you're not the only one anymore; there's someone else in the equation whose needs you have to meet. You share your time, your money, your life with them and sometimes you give up a part of yourself for the sake of the union."

I wasn't sure I understood exactly where she was coming from. Some of it, I did.

"Kind of like what I assume our folks did," Rob said.

"I guess so," Sam replied.

* * * *

We pulled up in front of Jeffreys' house a few minutes later. He still kept it in fairly good condition, considering its age.

"I can't believe I'm gonna be laying eyes on the old geezer after so many years," Sam said, loosing her seatbelt and getting out of the car.

"Guess he'll be glad to see us," Rob surmised.

We all headed up the walkway toward the porch. The guys let me walk ahead, just like back in the day when we had something of importance to do and none of them wanted to take the lead. It always had to be Jase or me.

I rang the doorbell and we silently waited. Several moments went by before I heard footsteps approaching from the inside.

The door swung open and the guys and I looked from the other side at a stunned Mark Jeffreys.

"Jeffreys, it's so good to see you again," Sam exclaimed.

"What...what are you all doing here?" He was clearly surprised, but I couldn't tell for sure if it was in a good way or not.

Jeffreys was now in his eighties and appeared even frailer than he looked when I'd last seen him. He was very thin and walked with the assistance of a cane. However, he still had all his faculties, perfect hearing and eyesight, and was just as independent as he always had been.

"We're in town together for the very first time since leaving for college," I told him. "So, we thought we'd stop by and see how you were doing."

"Yeah," Rob said.

A few more moments went by, then Jeffreys stepped aside and said, "Well, come in."

Right then, I had the feeling he wasn't too thrilled about us being there, especially since I knew he wasn't much of a people person.

The living room was dark—not a single curtain had been drawn. We all sat down while Jeffreys took a seat in his old, rocking chair.

"We heard about Hugo, man, and we're really sorry," Rob said. "We know how much he meant to you."

"Yup. Old Faithful's gone. This September will make twenty years. Buried right there in the yard out back." He rested his cane on the floor beside the chair.

"How old was he when he passed away?" Sam asked. This time, she and Rob were sitting together and I was alone on the sofa.

"He was fifteen years old. Lived a good life...but not long enough," Jeffreys answered. I saw the sorrow on his face by the mere mention of his dog. He cleared his throat and glanced at of us. "So, what brings you kids back in town after having been gone for so long?"

Sam and Rob looked at me.

"You remember our friend, Jase, don't you?" I asked.

Jeffreys rested his hands on his lap and interlaced his fingers. "I do."

"Well, we never found out what happened to him and his mom the day everyone was released from the compound," I explained. "After I moved away, I called the police department a number of times to find out if they'd found out anything, but it was useless. I don't think they were ever investigating the matter. One officer told me it's likely they both picked up and left town, but I knew that was impossible because they never returned to their house for any of their belongings. When the three of us here went to Jase's house after the spacecraft had left, their clothes, furniture—everything were still there. Weeks later—the same thing. Months went by and the place was untouched. Eventually, the bank repossessed it, then sold it two years later. I heard the furniture and appliances were offered at auction and the clothes left there were either thrown out or donated to charity. We know, without a shadow of a doubt, that Jase and his mom never left town. Something happened to them and we're here to find out what that is."

Jeffreys always had a naturally stoic expression; wasn't moved by much, other than his love for Hugo, but that day, he seemed *concerned*.

"I agree, the events are quite strange," he noted. "I can't imagine what might've transpired. Everyone else was accounted for that day when the nightmare was finally over."

"We agree," Sam chimed in. "And that's what we can't understand. They were the only captives who didn't return home. Yet, everyone had been released."

"Is there anything you can remember that stood out that day when they all got back?" Rob asked him.

Jeffreys thought for moment. "Nothing at all. Spader, Hugo and I went to the compound; had a meeting with the mastiff who promised to release everyone, and after we got back, at the exact time he said everyone would be back at home, they were. That's what I remember."

Some moments of silence ensued.

"Did Hugo say anything significant that might've been a clue of what happened to Jase and his mom?" I asked.

"You mean...before everyone around was *normal* again?" he asked.

"Yes."

"Nothing at all. Hugo told me everything when he had the ability to communicate with me the way we're communicating now. He didn't hide anything at all from me. So, no—he didn't say anything that could've been helpful because he was totally unaware of their whereabouts."

I must admit I was a bit disappointed that Jeffreys could not be of help even though I hadn't arrived with my hopes up.

"I'm sorry," he added.

"Thanks, anyway," I replied.

Jeffreys reached for his cane, then slowly stood up. "If that's all, I must get back to reading the newspaper and pouring my second cup of coffee for the day. I tend to do things in a timely fashion, if you know what I mean."

"We completely understand." Sam stood as well; Rob and I followed her lead. "It was good seeing you again."

"Likewise," he said, as he led us to the door.

It was sort of an awkward moment for us, despite being accustomed to Jeffreys' behavior.

"See you around," Rob said as we stepped onto the porch.

Jeffreys replied with a single nod.

"Well, that was a complete waste of time," Rob muttered after we got in the car. "I can tell nothing much has changed with that man."

"I have to agree," Sam said. "Didn't seem glad to see us at all and to think after we were on the same team for survival all those years ago, I thought we'd broken the ice once and for all.

"Guess that ice is impossible to crack."
Rob started the car, then pulled away.

6

The guys and I knew that if Hartley Mays, our town's former police chief, hadn't mellowed over the years it was highly unlikely he'd entertain us even for a minute. None of us were any of his favorite people and he certainly wasn't a fave of ours. Yet, he was instrumental back then in carrying out the wishes of the canines and so was every member of his police force. I realized they didn't have any choice in the matter, but the least they could've done over the years was to do whatever was in their power to find out what happened to two of our own.

The canines had sorely criticized us not only for failing to treat their kind with better care, but also for us not being our brother's keeper. I was wondering if anything had sunken into Chief Mays' heart concerning the latter. Rob had found out that he was retired now and living out the rest of his days in a nursing home after having suffered two heart attacks. His late wife's poodle, Dolly-Ann, just like Hugo, had long since passed and Mays was now on his own, sharing a similar fate to that of Mark Jeffreys. The difference between the men was that Jeffreys loved his dog and Mays didn't. Mays certainly *respected* her, if only that, after the traumatic events of 1995. Only a fool would've risked another visit from outer space.

"What if we can't get anything out of the guy?" Rob asked as we headed for *Green Pastures Nursing Home*.

"Have some faith, bro." I said.

Sam sighed. "We'd just have to cross that bridge when we get there, huh?"

"Hey. What about your dad's friend, Joe, who's a cop?" Rob asked me.

"Joe and his family left Eppington years ago right after everything returned to normal. His wife, Sandy, was so traumatized, she persuaded him to quit his job and leave town for good. Dad rarely heard from him ever since."

"Can't blame them for getting outta here," Sam remarked. "I can never understand why anyone stayed."

"Imagine an entire town picking up and leaving," I replied. "That'll make international news, for sure. It just couldn't happen. Besides, most people find it hard to uproot their lives and start all over again in a strange place."

"I did and it wasn't hard for me," she said.

"Everyone's not like you, Sam," Rob reminded her.

We arrived at the nursing home and it was agreed that I would go in and speak with Chief Mays alone instead of all of us crowding his space, even if more than one person was allowed to visit. The guys decided they'd wait in the lobby instead of outside running the car's A/C.

Chief Mays and Jeffreys were close in age, but Mays, being five years younger, looked nothing like I'd remembered; I hardly recognized the man. He used to be heavyset, around five feet eleven. Now, the person who sat in a chair looking out the window of his private room at the beautiful landscape was barely a hundred and twenty pounds and had lost a few inches in height as well.

"Is that really you, Spader?" He asked in a feeble voice, looking at me intently.

"It's me, sir." I sat next to him and tried to conceal my utter shock.

"I knew you'd come, sooner or later. 'Course, was no telling whether it'd be while I was alive or dead. You've made it."

I forced a smile. "How have you been?"

I quickly deemed it a stupid question.

"Not so good. This old body seemed to go downhill ever since…"

He started coughing.

"Are you all right? Should I get a nurse?"

He slowly raised a hand. "No. I'm fine."

He didn't look fine at all. In fact, he looked terrible. I was kind of feeling guilty for even being there bothering the guy.

"I know why you're here, Spader. No need to explain," he said. "You wanna know what happened to your friend and his mother."

"That's right." I felt my heart rate slowly increasing, now certain that Mays knew something all these years that he was finally ready to share.

"I'm sorry about what happened." He started coughing again. And again, I was concerned. This time, it lasted a little longer than the first bout. He reached up and wiped the corner of his mouth with a tattered handkerchief, then cleared his throat.

"One of my officers who was working at the compound said after you, Mark Jeffreys and his dog had spoken to the mastiff, he overheard a conversation between a couple of canines and apparently it…"

His voice started to drag.

"…it was agreed that…"

Suddenly, he held the left side of his chest and his face distorted in pain. He tried to get more words out, perhaps, a cry for help, but he obviously couldn't. I hurried out of the room, hollering for assistance when some nurses and a doctor rushed into the room and one of them ordered me out. As I was leaving, I noticed Mays was no longer struggling; the hand once holding his chest had fallen limp onto his leg.

I knew…he was dead.

* * * *

"What did you do to the guy?" Rob whispered loudly on the way to the car after a nurse had informed me of Mays' passing.

"I didn't do anything, Rob!" I answered defensively. "The guy died of a heart attack."

"Oh. I thought you'd held him at gunpoint to extract intel."

"Very funny." I shook my head. "He was on the verge of telling me…"

"Telling you what?" Sam held my arm, stopping me in my tracks. She had that look in her eyes I hadn't seen since we were kids—the look that said she knew I was on to something and she was dying to know what it was.

"He was about to tell me what happened. Started giving me a story about a conversation one of his officers who worked at the compound had overheard pertaining to some agreement."

"Agreement? Between who?" Sam grimaced.

I shook my head, hopelessly. "I don't know. That's when he had the attack."

"Bummer!" Rob exclaimed. "We were so bloody close!"

"Yeah." I nodded.

"Can you deduce anything from what he said," Sam pressed. "I mean…"

"I know what you mean and I thought about it over and over again as they were in there trying to save his life, but the answer is no. I have no idea what he was about to tell me—not even if Jase and his mom are dead or alive. Why did Mays have to drop dead right then?"

I knew that didn't sound very kind, but I was frustrated. Mays clearly had the answers we needed and had concealed them for decades. In the years I'd kept in touch with him to find out if they'd come across any clues pertaining to Jase's disappearance, not once did he let on that he knew anything. Now, when he was just a shell of the man he used to be, he was ready to unburden himself and I was angry about that. Why couldn't he find it within himself to do so sooner? Why did he keep what he knew under wraps for so long? How could that possibly have benefitted him—if it did at all?

"At least you tried," Sam said. "The question now is who is the officer Mays was referring to and do any of the other officers who were employed at the time share Mays' secret?"

"There's only one way to find out," I replied as we continued toward the car.

7

Sam had an engagement with her folks that she couldn't break, so we decided to call it a day and resume our investigations the next day.

When I arrived home, Carl was in the living room watching TV with his feet crossed on the center table. He was eating a super-sized club sandwich.

"You know Mom would've killed you if you ever parked your feet up there," I said, shutting the new screen door he'd installed that day.

"Mom's not here anymore," he answered, dryly.

"I know." Sitting on the sofa, I looked his way. "Still working out there or you're done for the day?"

"Not done." He kept his eyes on the TV.

"I meant to ask how your lunch date went yesterday."

"Same as usual." He took another bite of his sandwich.

"I see."

"Uncle Charlie called earlier. I didn't tell him you were here 'cause he would've wondered why he hasn't seen you yet."

"Thanks for that. I intend to walk over there this afternoon."

A wrestling match was on television and Carl was a huge fan. Yet, that day, he didn't seem as enthusiastic about it as he usually was.

"Hey, Carl…tell me—did I do something to upset you or…"

That's the first time he looked my way since I'd arrived.

"Upset me? You can't upset me, bro."

"Okay!" I threw my hands up. "If you wanna act like a spoiled child instead of talking it over like an adult, have it your way. I'll be out of your hair soon enough since it's looking like my trip was in vain anyway!"

I got up to leave.

"Wait!" He put the remnant of his sandwich on the table and muted the television.

As I slowly assumed my previous position, I noticed he was gathering his thoughts. He then turned to me.

"You want me to tell you what's on my mind, big brother? Well, I'll tell you. It was bad enough that you moved away and left us here after you know what Mom, Dad and I had gone through."

"Hold up!" I interjected. "What *you guys* went through? What about me and what I went through to rescue you—*all of you*—everyone in this blasted town? You think it was easy for me? It was horrifying knowing what had happened to you guys, wondering if I'd ever get you back and at the same time fighting to rescue you without being caught."

"I'm not saying you didn't go through anything, Hewey. I'm trying to say after it was over, you were a visitor popping in here and there. Mom missed you a lot and even though she never said she wanted you to come back home, I knew she did."

I shook my head. "You know Mom and Dad heard from me every other day and I saw them as often as I could. For goodness' sake, I'm a grown man! Mom knew I had to live my own life wherever I felt I needed to be. She never would've been selfish to lay a guilt trip on me about coming back home."

Looking at my brother, I knew he hadn't yet gotten to the crux of the matter.

"All those years of seeing me, Carl, you never once acted the way you've been acting since Mom and Dad died. We were always close, despite the distance between us. You used to call me all the time, then the calls got fewer and fewer and then stopped altogether. If I don't call you, you won't call. Something must've happened to change the relationship we had."

He was silent for a while, just sitting there shaking his head. Then the tears started streaming down his face.

"After Mom and Dad died, you abandoned me, Hewey."

"How?" I asked, completely stunned by his assertion.

"I had to be here handling their loss by myself in this house with all the memories. I didn't have anyone; no friends I could confide in about my true feelings—no one. I was all alone with my thoughts, crying my eyes out every single day for close to a year. For months, I kept Mom and Dad's bedroom door shut to prevent myself from going further into depression." He looked at me with a mixture of sadness and anger in his eyes. "When we were younger, you were the one with all the friends. In my mind, you, Mom and Dad were not just my family—you were my friends. So, when they were gone and you were so far away, I had nobody. And what's worse—you never came back after the funeral. After a year went by and you hadn't returned, I made up my mind that I had to find a way to cope on my own without you as a brother because you obviously didn't care about me enough to come back. And look—you're only here now because of your friend, Jase—and *I'm* your brother."

His words cut me to the core. I knew he was right about everything, but I'd never seen it that way before. "I had no idea you felt that way, Carl," I replied. "I knew losing Mom and Dad was really hard on you, especially since you were always here with them, but I guess I wasn't thinking straight. I was so wrapped up in my own grief that I couldn't bear to come back to this house because the reality that they were gone would've hit me way too hard. That's why I stayed away; not because I didn't want to see you or for us to be together like before. It was how I grieved and I was selfish about it, Carl, and I'm sorry. As your big brother, I was supposed to be here for you and maybe if I was, I would've been able to handle my grief a lot better."

I got up, went over to him and just stood there. Tears were still streaming down his face. "I'm sorry. I know I can't take anything back, but will you forgive me?" I asked. "I promise to be here for you even more than ever before." If he decided he'd rather not have anything more to do with me, I'd understand, but in my heart, I meant every word of what I said.

Moments later, he stood up and gave me the biggest hug ever and we were both in tears.

* * * *

I was relieved that Carl and I had finally broken the ice. Other than Uncle Charlie, he was the only family I had that was worth the definition of one.

That evening, Carl walked with me to Uncle Charlie's house where we ate a big bowl of peas soup only Uncle Charlie could make so perfectly.

Uncle Charlie was our mom's brother. He'd taught most of us in the neighborhood how to fish and often rented his canoes out. Nothing much had changed with him, except, like many of our neighbors, he'd also aged quite a bit. Uncle Charlie was hitting seventy-three and still going strong. He'd never married, but had a daughter who lived in New Jersey, whom he hardly ever saw. I don't think she and I had ever met and I wasn't sure if we ever would. Uncle Charlie was convinced her mother had filled her head with nonsense when it came to him, failing to tell his daughter how he'd fought for custody of her when she was a year old and lost because the judge thought he was bum since he was out of work at the time. Uncle Charlie only had so much fight in him. He thought the system was against him and that he was fighting a losing battle, so when his ex-girlfriend picked up and left with their child— moving to a whole new state—and made it close to impossible for him to see his baby by threatening to have her jailbird brothers beat him up, he figured he'd keep his distance and hoped his daughter would one day look for him. So far, that day never came.

"I thought you'd never come back here, boy!" He told me at dinner. "Three years is a long time to stay gone."

"Yeah. I was wrong for that." I glanced at Carl.

"I don't need you gettin' in your head that you're high society since you own that company in New Mexico," Uncle Charlie added. "No matter how far you climb up the ladder of success, you're still a small-town boy who used to piss his pants up to the age of twelve."

I was shocked he said that last part.

Carl was laughing.

"Well—you know where I got the information from. Your mother—of course! She told me everything about you boys."

"I'm sure she did," I mumbled. "You don't have to worry about my head getting all swollen, Uncle Charlie. Although I like to make money, I'm not controlled by it."

"Well, send some of it this way!" He swallowed a spoonful of soup.

"Haven't I always sent you money when you said you needed it?"

"Sure, you did. I'll always be grateful for the new canoes you bought to replace the old ones, but my bank account could always use a li'l boost every so often." He smiled.

"You're a piece a work, Uncle," Carl said.

"Am I, boy? Your brother knows I'm pullin' his leg."

I picked up my soda and took a gulp. "Uncle Charlie knows whenever he needs me I'm just a phone call away."

"I know that." He nodded. "Just like your folks knew. You're a good boy. Both of you are. Carl here took good care of them, especially when they were gettin' up in age. Never left their side and tended to their every need, And you, Hewey, did what you could from where you were at, and by all accounts, that was a lot. I told ya I know everything that went on. Your folks loved you two more than words could say and they were so proud of both of you."

He started to get a bit choked up, then quickly abandoned the topic.

"How about we go fishing on the lake?" I suggested.

"Today?" Uncle Charlie grimaced.

"Yeah. Right now. Carl, are you in?"

"I'm in." He rested his napkin next to his empty bowl.

"Well, I'm out!" Uncle Charlie said, dropping his spoon. "I'm full, I'm tired and I'm going to bed very early tonight."

"Well, have it your way," I said. "Olivia, here we come."

"You know where to put the dinghy when you're through," he said.

"Yeah—exactly where we found it," I assured him.

Those were our uncle's famous words. He'd once told us he'd written his will and had left everything to Carl since his daughter supposedly didn't want to have anything to do with him. He told me I didn't need what he owned because I could afford his estate a hundred times over. Regardless, the man had a good heart and he only did what he felt was right or fair, despite how truly wrong or unfair a situation might've been.

Carl and I spent a couple of hours fishing at Lake Olivia, catching a couple of tiny ones and tossing them back each time. Sam, Rob, Jase and I had spent many days on the lake in one of Uncle Charlie's dinghies, but Carl was often left out of the equation because he preferred playing video games instead. I figured my little brother and I had some catching up to do and we couldn't have asked for a nicer evening. It was cool out and the water was calm, glistening in the setting sun.

"From what you mentioned earlier, sounds like you guys are not making much headway finding out what happened to Jase, huh," Carl said, throwing his line back into the water.

I told him what happened to Mays and how Jeffreys was no help.

"We plan on going to the police station tomorrow to ask some questions. Hopefully, we'd uncover something there," I said.

"Maybe you guys should speak to the people who were closer in proximity to Jase and his mom when they were in the compound," he suggested.

"I hadn't thought of that, but I have no idea who they are."

"The Coopers around the block—one of Sam's neighbors—shared a cell with them. I remember that."

"Are you sure?"

"One hundred percent. They would've been released at the same time, so they should know something."

"Why didn't you tell me this sooner?" I frowned.

"You never asked! And to be honest, I never thought about it before now," he said.

"Well, that's definitely an avenue we must check out. Once that cell door was opened, they might've seen where Jase and his mother went—at least, in what direction."

"Hope it works out," Carl said.

"Thanks, li'l bro."

8

The following morning…

I called Sam and Rob and told them what Carl had said about the Coopers. Rob told me he'd pick me up around ten o'clock and we'd meet at Sam's house.

When Rob and I arrived there, Sam was standing on the front porch waiting for us. She hurried over to the car as we were getting out.

"No time to waste, guys. Let's get this thing done," she said.

That day, Sam was wearing a pair of cropped jeans, a beige tank top and navy-blue sports cap. She couldn't be more casual or sexier, in my opinion. My heart was throbbing for the girl and I pleaded inside for us to go back in time when we were just teenagers where I'd profess my love for her and she'd have no choice but to fall head over heels in love with me. At least, that would've been the ideal chain of events. Instead, I was stuck in the present, twenty-odd years later, wishing I'd told her how I always felt about her. Nevertheless, I had to get my head out of the cloud of regret and delusions. We had a case to solve that involved our best friend.

Sam's folks were not at home at the time; she claimed they'd gone in search of new plants for the garden. Their yard was still the envy of the entire neighborhood and I should've figured Mr. and Mrs. Turner wouldn't have left that property no matter what happened, especially after they'd put so much love into it.

"Hopefully, your folks wouldn't have this car towed away if they get back here before we do," Rob told Sam.

"Nah. Once they see the license plates, they'll figure it's your rental," she replied.

We immediately headed up the street on foot since the Coopers' house was only a few doors over.

"Sam, I think it's best you take the lead with them since they're your neighbors," I said.

"Okay, no prob."

The Coopers' house was a bit rundown with faded paint peeling in certain areas of the exterior wall, and the lawn was overgrown. I figured either they weren't doing so well financially or someone stopped giving a damn for whatever reason. A white sedan was in the driveway.

We walked up to the front door and after pressing the bell that didn't work, Sam knocked.

Seconds later, the door swung open and a young man appeared on the other side of it. He looked like he'd just rolled out of bed.

"Can I help you?" he asked.

"Hi. Good morning," Sam started. "I'm Sam Turner, your neighbor from down the street, and these are my friends, Hewey and Rob."

"I don't care who you are," he replied, nonchalantly. "What do you want?"

I assumed he was the Cooper's son, Max. I remember when he was a baby being carried around in the food store, strapped to his father's chest. I don't know what went wrong with him over the years, but something certainly did based on that attitude he was displaying.

"Is your Mom or Dad home?" Sam asked.

"Mom's asleep and…"

"Max…who is it?" A man called out.

"It's one of the neighbors and some other guys!" he yelled. "Asking for you and mom."

An older man suddenly appeared next to him. It was Mr. Cooper.

"Hi, there. How are y'all doing?" he said.

Seemed like the guy had only aged five years since I'd last seen him decades ago. He was clean cut and still quite handsome.

"We're fine, thanks." Sam smiled. Rob and I hailed as well. "We were wondering if we could speak with you for a moment."

"Sure. Come on in and make yourselves comfortable," he said.

The man and his son were like night and day.

Despite the shabbiness of the exterior of the house, inside was very nice and well-kept. The three of us sat together on the couch, although we figured Mr. Cooper wouldn't bite. We weren't so sure about Max though, who soon disappeared down the hallway.

"May I offer you some coffee or tea?" Mr. Cooper asked.

"No, thanks." We all responded.

He sat down across from us. "So, now, what can I help you with this morning? I guess, first of all, I should say that I recognize each of you. I remember when you were young kids riding your bicycles throughout the neighborhood; getting into some mischief here and there."

We all glanced at each other with a guilty smile.

"Yep…that's us," Sam replied. "Who can ever forget, huh?"

He grinned. "I can't cast any judgment on you guys since I was no saint as a kid either. I got into so much trouble, my folks threatened to take me to juvenile court."

"Really?" I was stunned. He seemed like such a calm, good-natured guy. I couldn't imagine that he was ever a pain in anyone's butt.

"Yeah. It's true. As I got older, I settled down a lot and decided it was best to do things my parents' way since the other way was causing far too many problems." He chuckled. "I got myself together just before I went to college, so that it wasn't likely I'd go off to a new state and get arrested over there."

We had a good laugh about it. Funny how people can look so innocent and have a darker side to them. I guess it's true for all of us.

"Okay, so now since that's out in the open, what can I do for you folks?"

Sam replied, "We all came back home this week because we want to try and find out what happened to our friend, Jase, and his mom. They haven't been seen since you all were held captive in the same cell at the compound many years ago and we're at a loss for answers."

Suddenly, Mr. Cooper's expression changed and he abruptly stood up. "I can't help you; I'm sorry. So, if you don't mind, I'll have to show you to the door."

I got up as well. "Wait...what the hell just happened? Why don't you wanna talk about it?" I asked.

"Because I don't know anything!" He stressed. "And I'd rather keep the whole horrible experience in the past. I will not speak of it."

"Sir…" Sam sought to interject.

"Please! Leave now or I'll have to call the police!"

Rob and I glanced at each other in sheer amazement. This guy was like Mr. Jekyll one minute and Mr. Hyde, the next.

"Maybe you should call the police!" Rob exclaimed. "Then we'll probably get to the bottom of what's going on around here sooner than we thought."

By this time, Mr. Cooper's eyes were glaring at us behind his clear, circular glasses. "Look...I don't want any trouble. I am being honest with you when I tell you I don't know anything; I have no idea what happened to your friend and his mother. The only thing I could think about while there was the safety of my wife and newborn child. I was grateful when it was all over and I don't want to relive it!"

"Well, we're the reason you're standing here today with the freedom you so cherish, Mr. Cooper." Sam told him. "If we hadn't found a way to rescue everyone in this town, you'd still be under the spell of the canines or worse, buried in that massive hole they intended to put you all in. The least you can do is tell us what happened to our friend if you have any idea at all."

"I don't," he said, stoically. "I appreciate whatever you've done—and now again, I'm asking you to leave."

The guys and I looked at each other, realizing this was another waste of our time, so we headed for the door. Cooper was already there.

"I saw them," went a soft voice behind us. It was Mrs. Cooper. She was standing with Max in the hallway. She looked haggard and worn—at least a good thirty years older than her husband, though in actuality, I knew she was at least a couple of years younger than he was.

Her husband hurried over to her. "Sheila, go back in the room and lie down."

"Let her speak!" Sam yelled.

She shoved her husband's hand away from hers and proceeded over to us. "You were right—that boy and his mother shared a cell with us," she spoke slowly. "Even though we couldn't communicate with each other, we were aware of what was going on around us and it was terrifying."

"Sheila..." Mr. Cooper called.

"Stephen, please leave me alone. I'm tired of being hush hush about this. It's been so long and not facing the trauma of what we went through is slowly killing me. Can't you see that?" Right then, she turned and gave him her full attention. "While ignoring the past has been working for you, keeping you looking young and healthy, do you see what it's done to me? Can't you see how terrible I look? I couldn't go anywhere without being afraid I'd be abducted or *controlled* again the way that we were. So, I stayed at home for twenty-four years. I don't know what the inside of the grocery store looks like where we went shopping all the time; I lost the job I loved which was teaching primary school kids; I lost my own identity—the person I was before that horrid spacecraft hovered above this town. No more, Stephen! No more."

She then turned to us again.

"Your friend and his mother were escorted out of that cell ahead of our release. A canine guard came to get them and said they were going to who they called *leader* and they never returned to the cell. I saw you there..." she pointed at me. "It was sometime after you'd left that the guard came and got them, and following them was a human guard."

I stepped closer to her. "Do you know what they did to them, Mrs. Cooper?"

"I don't, but I'm sure police constable Luke Barry would know. At least, that was his position at the time. He was the human guard I saw walking with them."

Breathing a sigh of relief, I reached out and held her hands. "Thanks so much, Mrs. Cooper. Bless you for finding it in your heart to tell us the truth."

She only nodded.

As we were leaving, Mr. Cooper hurried over to get his wife while their son leaned against the wall in front of the hallway, smoking a cigarette.

"Can you believe that?" Rob exclaimed, outside. "This woman was an answer to our prayers!"

"Yes indeed." Sam smiled.

I was jumping up and down in my head, thrilled at the progress we were finally making, but I knew it was too early to celebrate.

"We have a name, guys, and that's a great start, but we don't know what's coming, so contain your excitement because we're just getting started.

"I agree, Hewey," Sam replied. "But I'm overjoyed right now and I can't help it! After nearly thirty years, we finally have the name of someone who might know what happened to our friend." Her eyes welled with tears and I couldn't help but to stop and hold her.

"I know. I know, Sam."

Rob was walking a few feet ahead, giving us our space.

"Okay..." Sam dried her eyes with the back of her fingers. "I don't cry easily, but..."

"It's good to let it out," I said, quietly. "We all want nothing more than getting the answers that have evaded us for so long, and by some shred of hope, to see Jase and his mom again."

"Yeah."

"Let's find this constable now, shall we?" I smiled.

"Yep." She smiled back.

9

After phoning police headquarters in hopes of locating Constable, now *Chief Superintendent* Luke Barry, I was told he was on vacation and due back to work the following Monday. It was Thursday, which meant the guys and I had to find something productive to do until we got our shot at speaking with the officer.

Being *productive* meant hanging out at Rob's hotel and having a dip in the pool, *like tourists*, as Rob proudly put it; fishing on Lake Olivia in one of my uncle's dinghies like we used to do so many years ago; frequenting the local restaurants we couldn't afford to eat at when we were kids, and definitely sitting down for a couple of scoops of our favorite ice cream at Fredricka's Diner. However, the ice cream stop didn't happen until Saturday.

Even though I made sure to invite my brother, Carl, to hang out with us, he always declined and said Tamara was much better company. I was beginning to think he was getting quite serious about that girl. Did I hear wedding bells a little ways off in the future?

The Forresters had made some very attractive renovations to Fredricka's Diner since the building was now very old. The bright red fish scale shingles and wide fluorescent green overhang which had a plastic, animated look to it were still there. The walls had a radiant orange hue and they'd extended the building another forty feet to include more tables and chairs. Grandma Jane, who'd worked there well into old age had passed on and now the grandchildren, including former prom queen, Dale Forrester, who went to school with me were keeping Grandma Jane's dream alive.

Dale, whose beauty had not faded over time, had a short chat with the guys and me after we'd walked in. She was certainly more sociable than she was when we were kids.

As we sat there, revisiting our teenage years, Sam went on and on with Rob about how much he used to annoy her when we were hiding out in the distillery trying to find a way to rescue our folks. And, of course, he hadn't the slightest clue what she was talking about.

"I could've strangled you!" she barked. "We're in the crux of survival and you could never get your mind off that stomach of yours! You were a mess, Rob!"

"He's still a mess." I chuckled.

At our age, it was kind of hilarious watching them go at it, but back then, I had to step up as peacemaker. Otherwise, Sam might've torn off his head.

She looked at me. "Do you remember when he came into this same place for something to drink and walked out with a bunch of pastries instead?"

"I did get the ginger ale too!" Rob reminded her. "A few extra items wouldn't have hurt."

"They *might've* when we were in a hurry to get back to the hiding spot!" Sam shook her head as she clearly realized trying to convince Rob that focusing on his sweet tooth instead of survival was nonsensical.

Then he said something else that got her fired up and they were at it again.

That's when I noticed who'd just walked into the diner and was heading over to a table several feet away.

"Guys…guys…" I whispered under my breath. But, of course, they didn't hear me.

"Guys!"

Sam looked at me. "What?"

"Over there," I said, quietly keeping my focus straight ahead at the latest patron. Sam and Rob were now following my stare.

"Well, I'll be damned," Sam muttered. "If it ain't Mr. Clyde Rivera, former Bible-totin' adulterer and convict."

"He's out already?" Rob was stupefied.

"It's been twenty-five years or thereabout, bud. Guess he's done his time," I said.

"Well, I think they should've at least thrown away the key since they didn't give the guy the death penalty," Sam asserted. "He killed a whole woman! Both he and Mrs. Christie were wrong for cheating on their spouses, but the woman didn't deserve to die—and certainly not by his hands."

"Where's the justice, huh?" I said. "Mrs. Christie's dead and this guy gets to go on with his life."

"Not right, man. To think he killed her just to keep her mouth shut…" Rob sighed. "Anyway, it is what it is."

Clyde Rivera had a rough appearance like that of a construction worker who'd spent many days in the hot sun. He used to have a softer look when he was in management at the insurance company he'd worked at before he managed to get himself into serious trouble. Mom had said his wife, Suzanne, had divorced him after he was convicted, sold their house and moved to a new town with a new man. So, when Clyde got out, there's a good chance he was on his natural own.

"You guys ready?" Rob asked. "I wanna get outta here."

Clyde's presence had dampened Rob's and Sam's mood, but I didn't see why they let it get to them to that extreme. Sure, what the guy did was terrible, but he was still a part of the community and people just had to accept that fact.

"I'm ready," Sam said.

Rob stood up, gathered our empty plastic bowls and took them to the trash bin.

Sam and I proceeded to the door.

"Hewey Spader…is that you?" I heard a voice behind me.

I turned and just as I thought—it was Clyde. "Hey...Mr. Rivera," I said.

He actually got up and came over, smiling and all.

"I can't believe it! Last time I saw you, you were a li'l brat living down the street from me!"

"Yeah, I was. Wasn't I?" I grinned.

Rob walked over and was about to head out without us.

"You remember my friends, Sam and Rob?" I asked Clyde.

I saw vertical wrinkles on his now sixty-something-year-old forehead suddenly become more pronounced. "This is Sam? Really? Oh...wow. You've changed a lot! You look so...ladylike."

Sam rolled her eyes. She was definitely not interested in engaging in any type of conversation with the guy.

"Oh, and yes—Rob. I remember Rob. You don't look like you've aged a day since I last saw you."

Rob nodded, opened the door and walked out. Sam followed him.

"Anyway, it was good seeing you, Mr. Rivera," I said.

"It was great seeing y'all."

He didn't seem moved that much by Rob and Sam's reaction to him. Maybe he was used to it.

"By the way, I got out of jail two years and nine months ago," he spoke softly. "Been doing maintenance work for the police department ever since. The new chief was kind enough to give me the contract even though they don't pay that well. But I'm able to keep up with my apartment rent, utilities and have something left over for food to carry me through, you know?"

"That's good."

I got the impression he wanted to talk, but I had mixed feelings about it.

"Well...I won't hold you up any longer. I'm sure your friends are anxiously waiting for you." He started to walk off.

Then I remembered something. "Mr. Rivera! Can I ask you a question?"

He looked back. "Sure. Anything."

For the sake of privacy, I closed the gap between us a little more. "That time when the spacecraft was here... were you under the spell like everyone else was?"

I'd asked because I always wondered how he managed to even think of killing anyone in a zombielike state. Everyone was literally stripped of their will back then.

He glanced around, then said, "We should talk outside."

"Sure."

Rob was behind the wheel of the car and Sam was sitting next to him, staring at us as we made our way over to the side of the building.

Clyde sighed deeply. "It's funny you asked me that question, Hewey, because no one else ever did even during my trial. The truth is...Johnette and I had a terrible argument the same day the spacecraft showed up; I happened to be at her place at the time. I wanted to break things off with her because I knew it was wrong what we were doing and I still loved my wife. On top of that, God was watching and I was feeling so guilty. She threatened to tell my wife and said she'd ruin my life. Out of anger, I told her if she did that, I'd kill her and I called her every filthy name in the book. Nothing I said seemed to faze her because she was angry too. Then, in the heat of the argument, we heard something outside just above us and Johnette hurried out to see what it was. I couldn't do that because I didn't wanna be seen leaving her house, so I stayed inside and peaked through the window. Johnette went into the street and was looking up at the sky. There was a strange buzzing sound that was so intense it started to hurt my ears; I had to grab a couple of towels and press them against my ears to drown out the sound. When I got back to the window to see what was going on, I saw everyone—all the neighbors—standing in the street and their eyes were so strange-looking like they were in some sort of daze. Then I saw the dogs and heard their voices, speaking just like we did and I got scared. There was no way I was going out there. I realized when I eased one of the towels away from my ear, that I no longer heard the buzzing sound. Not long after that, Johnette came back inside and she was totally different. She looked and acted like a zombie. Didn't say anything to me; just went about the house doing chores as if she didn't know me. I knew something was seriously wrong and that it had to do with whatever was out there and I was sure everyone else was affected just like her. I'm ashamed to say that even though I was scared and didn't know what was going to happen the minute I walked out the door, I saw it as my opportunity to silence Johnette once and for all."

He paused for a moment and I could see the guilt and perhaps, regret, in his eyes.

"So, I unlocked her back door, planning to return that night and use it as my entrance. I was determined I needed to get her out of my life because if she woke up from this daze, we were bound to pick up where we left off with the argument and threats."

"It was you I saw that night from the top floor of the distillery…" I told him.

"You saw me?" He seemed surprised.

"Uh-huh. 'Course, I didn't know it was you at the time because it was so dark out."

He went on to tell how something fell to the floor as he was hurrying out of the house after he'd stabbed Mrs. Christie. That must've been the crashing sound I'd heard which prompted Sam and me to go over to the house the next morning and check on her.

"But to answer your initial question…I was never under that spell everyone else was obviously under. I watched my wife, Suzanne, turn into someone I didn't recognize and there was nothing I could do about it. When the buses came to get everyone, I escaped through the back and hid in the bushes, only returning home hours later."

"So, you stayed there the entire time?" I asked.

"Yep. I almost lost my mind. I knew the day would come when all the food ran out and I'd made up my mind that I was gonna die right there all alone and probably deserved it after what I'd done to Johnette. I couldn't believe my eyes when Suzanne was back home and was her old self again. By then, I was at my wits end, down to my last morsel of food and riddled with guilt. After holding her for what seemed like forever, I confessed everything to her and had to see the pain in her eyes. She encouraged me to turn myself in and that's what I did. The rest is history."

Clyde's explanation of those events didn't change my view of him or what he did, but I appreciated his honesty. After we said our goodbyes and went our separate ways, I couldn't help but think the guy had really messed up a good thing he had going and was now paying the price. According to him, Mrs. Christie had threatened to ruin his life, but the fact of the matter was he did a great job at that on his own.

"What the hell took you so long?" Sam barked at me the second I sat in the car.

Rob, who usually kept his cool, told me how much of a dimwit I was for wasting precious time conversing with a guy like Clyde Rivera.

"I'm feeling the hate, guys," I said. "Where'd the love go?"

After taking a sip from my water bottle, I went on to share with them the conversation I had with Clyde and how he was unaffected by the spell from the UFO. At least, they found that bit of information interesting.

"And that's why he was able to kill Mrs. Christie!" Sam announced.

"Precisely—because he couldn't have done it under the so-called spell," I returned.

"Idiot, either way!" Rob said.

10

Carl took a stroll with me through our neighborhood that Sunday. There wasn't much else to do.

I went and paid a visit to a few of our elderly neighbors who weren't doing so well physically and a couple of others who were completely bedridden. Our neighborhood was an old one with lots of houses that were standing for at least a half of a century. Mrs. Miller's, two houses down from ours, was actually close to a hundred years old and so was she. She lived with her caretaker, Doris, who'd been hired by Mrs. Miller's only son David, to be there with her. David happened to pass away ten years earlier and Doris never left. He'd made financial provisions for his mother to continue to be cared for in the event he did not survive her. Smart guy.

Then on the corner were Velda Howard who had a bad case of arthritis and her husband, Ben. Those two managed all right on their own, having their groceries delivered and one of the kids on the block to come and do yard work every so often. I remember when the Howards were middle-aged and fairly strong, going on their jobs and minding their own business, for the most part. They were pretty close to mom and dad—even invited us over for birthday parties when their kids were young. I noticed many of the adult children around the neighborhood had moved out. Carl, and a few others, had never left the nest.

I whipped up a nice dinner for Carl and me and sent a plate over for Uncle Charlie. I wasn't much of a cook, but at times, the dish was edible. Carl said the yellow rice with veggies and baked salmon was delicious. I'd have to agree, since most of the seasonings I used made my job a whole lot easier. I hadn't heard any complaints from Uncle Charlie, so that was a good sign.

Later that night as we hung out in the living room, I said to Carl, "How would you like to open a mechanic shop in town?"

He looked at me curiously. "What do you mean?"

"I know you do your work here in the yard which is fine, but how would you feel about having your own shop in an area where there's lots of traffic which can mean a lot more business?"

"I thought about it once, but I can't afford any overhead expenses," he replied. "Rent and utilities these days are so ridiculously high for residences, so imagine commercial buildings."

"What if I alleviated the rent part?"

"What are you getting at Hewey?"

"I saw a vacant lot there on Furlough Drive and think it's a great location for a mechanic shop. I'd like to purchase it for you—

that is, if you want it. If not, you can look for something else and let me know."

I couldn't read the expression on his face after I'd said that, and for a moment thought that somehow, I'd insulted his intelligence.

"You'd do that for me—buy me a piece of property?" he finally replied.

"Sure, I would! You're my brother."

He shook his head. "I can't believe it."

"You're not interested?" I reluctantly asked.

"The heck I ain't! I know the land you're talking about on Furlough. It's the perfect location, for sure." He smiled.

"Great! Because I have the contract of sale in my room."

"What the hell? Are you serious?"

"Yep. A couple of days ago while I was out with Sam and Rob, I found out who owned the property and quickly learned the guy was about to put it up for sale; had already informed his attorney. So—long story short, I told him I was interested; he gave the attorney instructions for the contract of sale and here we are. Now that it's a go, I'll have the money wired from my bank and the property is yours!"

"I can't believe this, Hewey! You're amazing, man!" He got up and gave me the biggest bear hug ever.

When he decided to release me, I went to my room and showed him the contract.

"Whew! One hundred and fifteen grand!" He exclaimed. "I still can't believe this, man."

Carl must've been the happiest guy on the planet that day and seeing him like that was the greatest feeling.

"So, next, we can find an architect and have some plans drawn for your new mechanic shop," I said. "And don't worry, li'l bro, I'm gonna help you with the construction too."

He was washed in tears by then and I loved every second of it.

11

Monday finally came—the day Sam, Rob and I were patiently waiting for. Luke Barry was the topic of conversation every day since Mrs. Cooper mentioned his name. Turns out, he was stationed at police headquarters where Chief Mays had worked his entire career.

We arrived there at a quarter past nine and were relieved that the hour had come for us to put some serious questions to this officer.

"Keep your fingers crossed," I said before we walked inside the station. Sam and Rob immediately sat down while I enquired at the counter.

"Good morning. I'm here to see Superintendent Barry," I said to the slanky officer seated at the reception desk.

"What's the name?" he asked.

"Hewey Spader."

"Superintendent Barry's in a meeting right now, Mr. Spader. Can someone else assist?"

"It's very important that I speak with him personally, so I'll wait," I replied.

He had no objections.

As we sat quietly, time slowly ticked by and before we knew it, a full hour had passed. By then, another officer had relieved the first guy at the reception desk.

I got up and went over to the desk again. "Excuse me. My name's Hewey Spader; I'm here to see Superintendent Barry. Can you check to see if he's still in a meeting please?"

This guy barely looked up to acknowledge me, unlike his much younger colleague. He did, however, pick up the phone and enquire.

"A Hewey Spader's here to see him," he said to whomever was on the line. Then, he finally made eye contact with me. "Are those two with you?"

I glanced back at Sam and Rob who were looking our way. "Yes…they are."

Our plan was for me to speak with Barry alone, as we didn't feel the need for all of us to be there, similar to the arrangement we had concerning our visit with Chief Mays. But since the officer asked if the guys were with me, I was thinking that maybe there should be a change of plans.

The officer ended the call, slid a large black book with dogears in front of me and said, "Write down all of your names here."

I did as requested, then he directed me to enter the door directly behind him and offered further instructions on how to find Barry's office.

Luke Barry was in his mid-fifties, a bit on the tall side and clean-shaven. His head was as shiny as a bowling ball. Sipping a cup of coffee at his desk, he made a single gesture of his hand for us to have a seat when we arrived at the door.

We all said *good morning*.

Barry got up and extended a handshake to each of us. After returning to his chair, he asked, "How can I help you?"

Of course, neither Sam nor Rob bothered to respond.

"Sir, my name is Hewey Spader…"

"Yeah. I understand you had called for me late last week and were told I was on vacation, due back today. Very little happens around here, especially concerning me that I don't know about, Mr. Spader. Every phone call, every text, every email—I am aware of. What I want to know is why you're here."

I crossed my legs, assuming a more comfortable position. "I guess I should start by saying that my friends, Sam and Rob here, and I have a friend and his mother who have been missing for more than twenty-five years. We've gotten absolutely no answers and no indications from police that there have been leads or an investigation concerning the matter and we think it's high time someone showed some interest in finding out what happened to them."

"What's the name of the missing persons?" he asked.

"Jason and Catherine Anderson."

He nodded. "I remember those names."

"Has there been any type of leads in the matter?" I asked.

It took him a few moments to respond.

"I can't say for sure."

"Well, who can?" Sam interjected.

"If I can't tell you, there's nothing to tell," he replied.

"What kind of nonsense is going on around here?" Sam exclaimed. "How in the world can two people go missing from a small town like this and no one—absolutely no one gives a damn?"

She'd caught me off guard there, but I must say that I admired her spunk—always had.

Barry was silent.

"I went to see Chief Mays just before he died," I continued. "And he started to tell me something about an officer overhearing a conversation regarding Jase and his mom during that time when residents here were held captive on the compound…"

"Uh-huh," he muttered.

"And then another resident recently called *your name* indicating that you might know something about the disappearances and that's why we're here."

He was nodding again, but I could tell he was feeling rather uncomfortable.

"If you know something, sir, we would appreciate you telling us," Rob chimed in.

"Well, if we don't get our answers today," Sam started, "When I go home, I'll be contacting every major news station in this country and also in France where I live and I'm gonna make it known that law enforcement in Eppington has either failed to investigate or is covering up the matter pertaining to our friend and his mother's disappearance. And I guarantee you, sir, that some heat is gonna come down on this town like you'd never seen. A pity it didn't happen long ago!"

For the better part of a minute, we all sat there without uttering a single word. Barry was now looking more uncomfortable than ever.

Then he finally said, "Only three people know exactly what happened to the Andersons and one of them is dead. The fact is…he only knew the truth because I told him. He was my superior who I trusted back then with my life and we promised not to speak a word of it in case those aliens came back for us with a vengeance. But what ended up happening was it gradually became a burden for Chief Mays since his duty—all of our duty—was to serve and protect the people of this community. We hadn't done that for two of our own and keeping quiet about what happened to them that last day at the compound was extremely difficult to bear."

"You seemed to have coped with it all right," Sam asserted, much to my dismay. Sometimes, the girl just went overboard.

Barry slid open one of his desk drawers, then placed multiple prescription medication packets on top of the desk.

"Looks can be deceiving," he said. "This is how I cope with what I know. As a high-ranking police officer, it's embarrassing to say that the events of 1995 changed me to where I'm frightened even to this day and more so because of a secret I'm afraid to tell—but it's true. Chief Mays obviously tried to get it off his chest before he died."

I was startled by Barry's confession.

I remember you, Mr. Spader. I knew who you were from the moment you walked in here. I saw you at the compound that last day. You had a meeting with the Tibetan Mastiff leader of the canines, but what I overheard from two other canines was that those with you also had a private meeting with the leader while you were still there. What they went on to say is what I'm afraid to utter for fear that somehow those beings will hear and come back and retaliate against me and my family. I cannot risk that, Mr. Spader— I'd die first. What I suggest is that you get the truth out of the man who was directly involved and knows firsthand what really happened—and don't stop until you do."

He gave us the name that shocked us to the core, and without delay, we were on our way to confront him.

12

I banged on Jeffreys' door and didn't stop until he opened up. The anger I felt inside was something I hadn't remembered ever feeling before.

He soon opened the door with a confused expression on his face.

"How could you?" Sam demanded after we'd entered his house without an invitation.

"What are you talking about?" Jeffreys asked, clearly shocked by our hostile intrusion.

"Tell us what happened in that meeting the leader of the canines had with you and Hugo after I left the room," I insisted.

"What meeting?"

"You know what meeting I'm talking about, Jeffreys!" I scoffed. "After I went in there and he agreed to release everyone and leave this town, you and Hugo were called in. You made me believe it was all about him dealing with Hugo for betraying his own kind, but there was more to it than that, wasn't it? What didn't you tell me?"

"I have no idea what you're talking about, Spader."

He turned his back on me and sat down in his rocking chair.

I grabbed him by the collar. "You either tell me the truth, old man, or this face is gonna be the last one you'd ever see!"

He glanced at Rob and Sam as if they'd care to rescue him. I'm sure he remembered, according to his own words, how we were rascals and brats in our younger years. I'm guessing at that particular point in time, he figured not very much had changed.

I tightened my grip to show him I was dead serious.

"Okay! Okay!" He held up his hand. "I'll tell you."

I released him and he sat back in the chair.

"We're waiting!" Sam said.

Jeffreys sighed heavily. "It's best if you all sat down for this."

The guys and I glanced at each other and reluctantly sat with him in the living room.

It seemed like a century had passed before he spoke again.

"Spader, I hate to break the news to you that your agreement with the leader was not as cut and dry as you thought it was."

"What are you saying?" I was sitting at the edge of the chair.

"He called Hugo and me in there, yes—to scold Hugo about his betrayal of their kind for the sake of us humans, but also to tell us that because of his betrayal, there would have to be a trade-off. For him to release the residents of this town, two of them would have to go with them when they were leaving."

"What? We all exclaimed, simultaneously.

"A trade-off?" I said.

"Yes." He nodded slowly.

"He asked for names, and Hugo and I both hesitated for the longest time because we couldn't believe what he was proposing. However, he said it was the only way he'd release everyone. Two people had to be the sacrifice for an entire community was the way he put it. In the end, it was left for me to decide who those people should be since they were our kind."

I couldn't believe my ears. "So, you chose Jase and his mother?"

"I did."

"Why *them*?" Rob asked.

"Because the two people had to be someone close to you, Spader. It would've been either your parents or two of your friends; I'm sorry. I knew Jase only had his mother and figured if I chose them, no matter what happened, they'd be together."

Tears were streaming down Sam's sweet little cheeks again and Rob was teary-eyed too.

"I can't believe this," I whispered.

"The mastiff promised they wouldn't be harmed though," Jeffreys quickly added. "That's the only reason why I've been able to live with myself and this secret for so many years."

"Do you know what ever became of them?" Sam asked. "Did Hugo know?"

With the assistance of his cane, Jeffreys got up and walked into the hallway. I reached over and wrapped my arms around Sam's shoulder, trying to comfort her.

"This is crazy," Rob said. "Our buddy, Jase, turned out to be a victim in this situation more than once."

Sam nodded in agreement.

Jeffreys soon returned holding something in his left hand. He sat down again, then called us over.

"I want to show you all something," he said as we stood around him. The device he was holding resembled a miniature computer screen—approximately three inches on all sides—but this was unlike any computer I'd ever seen.

"What is this?" I asked him.

"This was handed to me by the mastiff before Hugo and I left his office. I was directed to conceal it on my way out. In light of what I had done, it was to offer me assurance that no harm had come to the boy and his mother."

He waved his wrinkled hand across the face of the device and it immediately lit up. We all leaned in, and to our surprise, saw a little wooden house surrounded by fruit-bearing trees, and on the porch was Jase's mom. She was sitting alone, shelling peas with a white bowl in her lap.

"Honey, come here!" she called out toward the door. And shortly thereafter, a tall, handsome man, clearly in his forties, joined her outside.

"It's Jase!" Sam declared, cheerfully.

"Yeah. It's him, isn't it?" Rob's face lit up.

"It's him all right." I was choked up, fighting back the tears. It was the very first time any of us had seen our friend for nearly thirty years.

"Where are they?" Sam asked Jeffreys.

"I have no idea," he replied. "That little detail was not disclosed to me. Over the years, I checked in on them periodically, but they can't see or hear me. They're always outside enjoying the fresh air, doing odds and ends, gardening and such."

"Have you ever seen anyone else with them?" I asked.

"Never. I have a feeling wherever they are, it's likely in the middle of nowhere."

Jase took the bowl of peas from his mom and kissed her on the cheek.

"In spite of everything, they seem happy," Sam said.

For a while, I was at a loss for words. The reality of the matter was taking its own slow time setting in.

"Why didn't you tell us, Jeffreys?" Sam asked. "You knew Jase was our friend and how concerned we were when we found out they were missing. Why did you keep this from us—at least the knowledge that they were alive?"

"Yeah. How could you?" Rob grimaced.

"I had to protect Hugo while he was still here," Jeffreys admitted. "Then, after he was gone, I felt I had to protect myself. Knowing what I'd done, it was easy to believe that if I told you kids what had really happened, you'd be furious, just like you were when you got here today. I'll be joining Hugo soon, so it doesn't matter that much anymore. It's all out now and honestly…I'm relieved."

I had mixed emotions about Jeffreys and what he had done. Sam and Rob did too. The truth, however, was that he was cornered to make a decision that would've affected others in a major way and at the time, he did what he thought was best.

We left his home that day knowing we'd probably never see the man again; neither did we want to.

As we headed to my house to hang out for a while, Sam held the device Jeffreys had turned over to us and watched lovingly while Jase's mom hummed softly in her little rocking chair as dust wisped into the air around the wooden house.

* * * *

"I'll be heading back home tomorrow since our mission here is accomplished," Sam said, as she and I sat alone on the back porch.

Carl and Rob were inside watching a football game and discussing what had been uncovered within the last couple of hours.

"When are you leaving?" she asked.

I shrugged. "I'm not sure yet. Think I'm gonna hang around here for a few more days and help Carl with getting a plan started for his mechanic shop."

"It's so nice what you're doing for your brother, Hewey. I'm sure he's thrilled about it."

"Yeah, he is. Haven't seen him so happy in a long time."

She smiled.

"I guess your husband can't wait for you to get back home."

She was staring straight ahead. "It's not like what you think. We're actually getting divorced."

I shook my head. "I'm really sorry, Sam."

"Don't be. It's been terrible for a long time and I just wanna get it over with."

I wasn't sure what to say.

"At one time, I thought he was my soulmate," she continued. "But I was so wrong."

I reached for her hand and squeezed it gently.

"I should've followed my heart."

"Where was your heart leading you?" I asked.

She turned and looked at me with those beautiful eyes of hers. "It was leading me here with you ever since I turned sixteen."

I was stunned. "Why didn't you say anything to me?"

"Because I was afraid of getting rejected. We were so close and I didn't want to risk the friendship we had," she explained.

"I wish you would have."

"What?"

I leaned over, held her face and kissed her passionately.

"I have been in love with you my entire life, Sam," I whispered. "I always knew you were my soulmate."

We kissed again, then held each other. And I wished that moment would last forever.

* * * *

The next day, Carl, Rob and I saw Sam off at the airport. It was nice having my brother with us for a change.

"So, you two are an item now?" Rob asked as we were pulling away in Carl's jeep.

"She's moving to New Mexico to be with me after the divorce has been finalized." I smiled.

"Splendid! I knew you two had the hots for each other from we were kids. I have no idea why people don't just tell each other how they feel so they wouldn't waste any precious years hooking up with people they never should've been with in the first place! Don't you agree, Carl?"

My brother laughed. "I think you have a point there," he said.

Rob's flight was scheduled for the following day. Carl and I spent the afternoon with him at his hotel having a few drinks and shooting the breeze. We had a great time together.

Rob and Sam entrusted me with the device Jeffreys had offered up to us and we all promised to keep in touch. We decided not to be intrusive upon Jase and his mother's space, but only to check in periodically to see if they were still there. I was amazed how it all worked out, but saddened by the possibility that our friend was gone forever.

However, we were thankful that he and his mother were still very much alive.

~ THE END ~

PLEASE LEAVE YOUR REVIEW ONLINE FOR THIS BOXED SET.

*AND KEEP READING FOR YOUR FREE EXCERPT OF ANOTHER BESTSELLING COZY MYSTERY SERIES.

Discover Lucille Pfiffer Mystery Series
*FREE EXCERPT **OF BLIND SIGHT***
to follow.

Lucille Pfiffer sees, but not with her eyes.
She lives with her beloved dog Vanilla in a cozy neighborhood that is quite "active" due to what occurred in the distant past. Though totally blind, she plays an integral role in helping to solve pressing and puzzling mysteries, one right after the other, which, without her, might remain unsolved.

The question is: How can she do any of that with such a handicap?

FREE EXCERPT OF *BLIND SIGHT*

1

Super Vanilla

I carefully descended the air-conditioned jitney and started down the sidewalk with my cane in hand and Nilla, my pet Shih Tzu on leash at my side. Taking a cab was our preferred mode of transport, but sometimes we enjoyed a nice, long bus ride instead. Nestled on both sides of the street were a number of shops, including convenience stores, jewelry, liquor, antique stores and haberdashery.

It was the day before my scheduled meeting with the local pet society that while walking along downtown Chadsworth, I heard a woman scream. The vision of her anguished face flashed into my mind and the image of a young boy dressed in faded blue jeans and a long-sleeved black shirt running at full speed in the direction Nilla and I were headed. Gripped tightly in his hand was a purse that did not belong to him; his eyes bore a mixture of confidence in his escape intertwined with fear of capture. He was quickly approaching—now only several feet behind us. In no time, he would turn the bend just ahead and be long gone bearing the ill-gotten fruits of his labor.

One could imagine how many times he'd done the same thing and gotten away with it, only to plan his next move – to stealthily lie in wait for his unsuspecting victim. I heard the squish-squashing of his tennis shoes closely behind. It was the precise moment he was about to zoom past us that I abruptly held out my cane to the left, tripping him, and watched as he fell forward, rolling over like a car tire, then ultimately landing flat on his back on the hard pavement. I dropped the leash and yelled, "Get him, Nilla!"

Nilla took off at full speed and pounced on top of the already injured boy, biting him on every spot she could manage – determined to teach him a lesson he'd never forget. He screamed and tried to push her off of him, but a man dashed over and pinned him to the ground. I made my way over to Nilla and managed to get her away from the chaotic scene. Her job was done. As tiny as she was, she made her Momma proud.

The frantic woman got her purse back and the boy was restrained until police arrived.

2

The room was almost packed to capacity when I arrived at the podium with the gracious assistance of a young man. As he went to take his seat in the front row, I proceeded with my introduction: "My name's Lucille Pfiffer—Mrs., that is—even though my husband Donnie has been dead and gone for the past four and a half years now. We had no children, other than our little Shih Tzu, Vanilla; 'Nilla' for short." I smiled, reflectively. "By the way, I must tell you she doesn't respond to 'Nill' or 'Nillie'; it's 'Nilla' if you stand a chance of getting her attention. She totally ignores you sometimes even when you call her by her legal name '*Va (vuh)*…nilla'.

"We reside in a quiet part of town known as Harriet's Cove. A little neighborhood with homes and properties of all sizes. We're mostly middle class folk, pretending to be upper class. The ones with large homes, much bigger than my split level, are the ones you hardly see strolling around the neighborhood, and they certainly don't let their kids play with yours if you've got any. Those kids are the 'sheltered' ones—they stay indoors mainly, other than when it's time to hop in the family car and go wherever for whatever."

I heard the rattle inside someone's throat.

"Uh, Mrs. Pfiffer…" A gentleman at the back of the room stood up. "I don't mean to be rude or anything, but you mentioned the neighbors' kids as if you can see these things you described going on in your neighborhood. I mean, how you said some don't play with others and they only come out when they're about to leave the house. But how do you know any of this? Or should we assume, it's by hearsay?"

I admired his audacity to interrupt an old lady while she's offering a requested and well-meaning introduction to herself. After all, I was a newbie to the Pichton Pet Society and their reputation for having some 'snobby' members preceded them.

"Thank you very much, sir, for the questions you raised," I answered. "Yes, you are to assume that I know some of this—just some—via hearsay. The rest I know from living in my neck of the woods for the past thirty-five years. I haven't always been blind, you know." I liked how they put you front and center on the little platform to give your introductory speech. That way, no eyes could miss you and you think, for one delusionary moment, that you're the cream of the crop. Made a woman my age feel really special. After all, at sixty-eight, three months and four days, and a little *over-the-hill*, I highly doubted there were going to be any young studs falling head over heels in love with me and showering me with their attention.

"Pardon me, ma'am." He gave a brief nod and sat back down again.

I took that as an apology. I could see the look on Merlene's face as she sat in the fourth row from the front. She thought I'd blown my cover for a minute there, but she keeps forgetting that I'm no amateur at protecting my interests. Sure, I sometimes talk a bit too much and gotta put my foot in my mouth afterwards, but my decades of existence gives me an excuse.

I could hear Merlene scolding me now:

"Lucille, I've told you time and time again, you must be careful of what you say! No one's gonna understand how an actual blind woman can see the way you do. They won't believe you even if you told them!"

Her words were like a scorched record playing in my brain. She got on my nerves with all her warnings, but I was surely glad I was able to drag her down there to the meeting with me that day.

I tried not to face that guy's direction anymore, even though the dark sunglasses I wore served its purpose of concealing my *blind stare*. "Thank you, sir," I said. "Well, I guess there's not much left to say about me, except that I used to have a career as a private banker for about twenty years. After that, I retired to spend more time with Donnie, who'd just retired from the Military a year earlier. We spent the next twenty-one years together until he passed away from heart trouble."

Someone else stood up—this time a lady around my age. "If you don't mind my asking…at what point did you lose your eyesight? And how are you possibly able to care for your pet Vanilla?"

When I revisit that part of my life, I tend to get a tad emotional. "It was a little over eight years ago that I developed a rare disease known as Simbalio Flonilia. I know, it sounds like a deadly virus or something, but it's a progressive and rather aggressive deterioration of the retina.

They don't know what causes it, but within a year of my diagnosis, I was totally blind. I'm thankful for Donnie because after it happened, he kept me sane. Needless to say, I wasn't handling being blind so well after having been able to see all of my life. Donnie was truly a life-saver and so was Nilla. She's so smart—she gets me everything I need and she's very protective, despite her little size. I've cared for Nilla ever since she was two months old and I pretty much know where everything is regarding her. Taking care of her is the easy part. Her taking care of me is another story."

Though somewhat hazy, I could see the smiles on many of their faces. The talk of Nilla obviously softened some of their rugged features.

Mrs. Claire Fairweather, the chairperson, came and stood right next to me.

"Lucille, we are happy to welcome you as the newest member of our organization!" She spoke, eagerly. "You have obviously been a productive member of Chadsworth for many years and more importantly, you are a loving mom to your precious little dog, Vanilla. People, let's give her a warm round of applause!"

A gentleman came and helped me to my chair. The fragrance he was wearing reminded me of how much Donnie loved his cologne. Such a fine man, he was. If it were up to him, I wouldn't have worked a day of my married life. It would've been enough for him to see me every day at home just looking pretty and smiling. His engineering job paid well enough, but I loved my career and since it wasn't a stressful one, I didn't feel the need to quit to just sit home and do nothing.

"Thank you, dear," I told the nice, young man.

"My pleasure, Mrs. Pfiffer."

Merlene leaned in as Claire proceeded with the meeting. "I told you—you talk too blasted much!" She whispered. "If you keep up this nonsense, they're gonna take your prized disability checks away from you."

"It'll happen over my dead body, Merlene," I calmly replied.

"Mrs. Pfiffer, I must say it's truly an honor that you've decided to join us here at the Pichton Pet Society," Claire said at the podium. "With your experience as a professional, I'm sure you'll have lots of ideas on how we can raise funds for the continued care of senior pets, stray dogs and abused animals. Your contribution to this group would be greatly appreciated."

After the meeting, she'd caught Merlene and me at the door, as we were about to head for Merlene's Toyota.

"I'm so glad you joined us, Mrs. Pfiffer. My secretary will be in touch with you about our next meeting."

"Thank you, Mrs. Fairweather. I'm honored that you accepted me. After all, animals are most precious. Anything that supports their best interest, I'm fired up for."

"Did you always love animals?" she asked.

I gulped. "Well, if I may be straight with you... I hated them— especially dogs!"

Her hand flew to her chest and a scowl crept over her face. I must have startled her by the revelation.

"It was after Nilla came into our life that I soon found a deep love and appreciation for animals—especially dogs. To me, they're just like precious little children who depend on us adults to take care of them and to show them love, as I quickly learned that they have the biggest heart for their owners."

Fairweather seemed relieved and a wide smile stretched across her face. "Oh, that's so good to know! I was afraid there for a moment that we'd made a terrible mistake by accepting you into our organization!" She laughed it off.

I did a pretend laugh back at her. I may be blind, but I'm not stupid—that woman actually just insulted me to my face!

"I don't know why you want to be a part of that crummy group with those snooty, snobbish, high society creeps anyway!" Merlene remarked after we both got in the car.

I rested my cane beside me. "Because I've been a part of crummy groups for most of my adult life. I don't know anything different."

Merlene gave me a reprimanding look. "It's not funny, Lucille. You dragged me out here to sit with people who, I admit love animals, but they seem to hate humans! I've heard some things about that Fairweather woman that'll make your eyes roll. You know she's a professor at the state college, right?"

"Uh huh."

"Well, I heard she treats the kids who register for her class really badly. She fails most of them every single term. The only ones who pass are the ones who kiss up to her."

"If there's a high failure rate in her class, why would the state keep her on then?" I asked.

"Politics. She got there through politics and is pretty much untouchable. I heard she also was a tyrant to her step-kids. Pretty much ran them all out of the house and practically drove the second fool who married her insane. He actually ended up in the loony bin and when he died, she took everything—not giving his kids a drink of water they can say they'd inherited."

"I blame the husband for that."

"Not when she got him to sign over everything to her in his will when he wasn't in his right mind. The whole thing was contested, but because she was politically connected, she came out on top. After that, she moved on to husband number three. If I knew that woman was the chairperson of this meeting you dragged me out to, I would've waited in the car for you instead of sitting in the same room with her."

We were almost home when Merlene finally stopped talking about Fairweather. You'd think the woman didn't have a life of her own, considering the length of time she focused on this one individual she obviously couldn't stand. I just wanted to get the hell out of that hot car (the two front windows of which couldn't roll down), and get home to my Nilla. She'd be waiting near the door for me for sure.

I wish I was allowed to bring her to the meeting. They claimed they're all about animals, but not one was in that room. I guess I was being unfair since they mentioned that particular Monday meeting was the only one they couldn't bring their pets to. That was the meeting where new members were introduced and important plans for fundraisers were often discussed.

"I'll see you later, Lucille. Going home to do some laundry," Merlene said after pulling up onto my driveway. "Need help getting out?"

"I'm good," I replied.

"How sharp is it now?"

"I can see the outline of your face. Nothing else at the moment. Everything was almost crystal clear in the meeting."

"Yeah. Inopportune time for it to have been crystal clear," Merlene mumbled.

She was used to my *inner vision*, as we call it, going in and out like that. I grabbed hold of my cane and the tip of it hit the ground as I turned to get out of the vehicle. "I can manage just fine. I'm sure it'll come back when it feels like. Thanks for coming out with me."

I smiled as I thought of how much she often sacrificed for me. Ten years my junior, Merlene was a good friend. We had a row almost every day, but we loved one another. She and I were like the typical married couple.

"By the way, I forgot to mention, my tenant Theodore, told me this morning that someone had called about renting the last vacant room."

"Perfect!" Merlene said.

"Said he was coming by this afternoon. What time is it?"

"It's a quarter of five."

I had an idea. "Merlene, he's supposed to show up at five o'clock. You wanna hang around for a few minutes to see what my prospects are? Maybe he's tall, dark and handsome and I may stand a chance."

"I doubt it," she squawked. "Besides, I must get at least a load of laundry done today. If not, I'll likely have to double up tomorrow for as quick as that boy goes through clothes! I tell ya, ever since he met that Delilah, he's changed so much."

"Why don't you leave that boy alone?" I barked. "He's twenty-seven-years-old, for Heaven's sake! Allow him to date whomever the hell he feels like. He's gotta live and learn, you know, and buck his head when need be. You and I went through it and so must he. You surely didn't allow your folks to tell you who you ought to date and who you shouldn't, did you? And furthermore, why do you keep calling Juliet, *Delilah*?"

"Because she's just like that Delilah woman in the Bible; can't be trusted!" Merlene spoke her mind. "And since you asked—why do you call her *Juliet*? Her name's Sabrina."

I sighed. "You know why I call her that."

"I tell ya...she's no Juliet!"

"Anyway, you're gonna wait with me a few minutes while I interview this newcomer or not?" I'd just had enough of Merlene's bickering for one day.

I heard her roll up the two remaining car windows and pull her key out of the ignition. It was one among a ring of keys.

Nilla was right at the front door when I let myself in. I leaned down and scooped up my little princess. She licked my face and I could feel the soft vibration of her wagging tail. Merlene walked in behind me.

"Nilla pilla!" she said, as she plonked down on the sofa. "Why can't you assist Mommy here with her interview? After all, you've gotta live with the newbie too."

I heard Theodore's footsteps descending the staircase. His was a totally different vibration from Anthony's. Anthony's steps were softer like that of a woman's feet. I had a good look at him a few times and he definitely was *Mister Debonair*. And that desk job he had at the computer company suited him just fine. Theodore was different; he was more hardcore, a blue collar worker at the welding plant, pee sprinkling the toilet seat kinda guy. That was my biggest problem with him – he wasn't all that tidy, especially in the bathroom. But I hadn't kicked him out already because he's got good manners and sort of treats me like I'm his mother. Anthony mostly stays to himself and that's fine with me too.

After I'd sat down, Nilla wiggled constantly to get out of my arms. She didn't like "hands" as much as she preferred dashing all over the place, particularly when her energy level was high. I could tell that was the case at the moment, so I gently let her down on the tiled floor and immediately saw her sprinting through the wide hallway which led into the kitchen, then doubling back into the living room seconds later, and making her way under the sofa. Under there was her favorite spot in the entire house. Often, she stayed in her hut-like habitat for hours at a time.

"Good evening, ladies," Theodore said as he entered the living room. How did the meeting go?"

"It was horrible!" Merlene replied.

"It went fine, Theodore. Beautiful atmosphere; beautiful people," I said.

"She got her fifteen minutes of fame," Merlene snapped. "That's all she cares about. She should've invited *you* to waste a full two hours there instead of me."

Theodore laughed. "Well, I'll be heading out to work. See you later."

"Yeah, later," Merlene replied.

As Theodore opened the door, he met someone standing on the other side. "Oh, I'm sorry. Almost bumped into you," he said.

Theodore went his way and the person stepped inside.

"What're you doing here, David?" Merlene asked.

"I'm here to see Miss Lucille. I'm interested in renting the room."

I could sense Merlene's shock. After all, why would her son who lives with her come to rent a room from me?

3

David had an air of innocence about him; he'd always been that way. He was more on the slim side, had dark hair and a cute dimple in his left cheek. He looked a lot like Merlene; her genes were obviously just as strong as her personality. That runaway husband of hers, Roy Bostwick, hardly injected any looks into their only child. I always thought Merlene's failed relationship with Roy had embittered her from ever investing in any new relationships since he upped and left her for a younger woman shortly after she retired as a school secretary. She'd spent just about all of her retirement money on expensive "man toys" like that convertible she had to fight him for in court after he'd left. Merlene was just never the same after the divorce. She went through her house on a daily basis, constantly looking for something to clean, or came over to my place to shoot the breeze, if we didn't have plans for an outing. That's of course, when she wasn't busy prying into David's personal affairs and trying to live her life through him.

"What are you talking about, David?" She sat straight up, suddenly finding the energy it took to do mounds of laundry when she got home.

"Mom, if you don't mind, I need to speak with Miss Lucille. You and I can talk later, okay?"

Merlene was stunned. Knowing her, she was also seething inside after being *casually* handled by her son.

"Miss Lucille, I called this morning, but was told you were in the restroom. I heard you have a vacant room for rent and was wondering if I can have it." He spoke with the humility of a saint. The boy was just so good. If I had children, I'd want them to be like him.

"Well, David... I don't know. I think you'd better discuss this with your mother. I really don't want to be placed in a situation where I must choose between my friend and her son." Although, in my mind, I was leaning more towards the boy. Maybe he only needed a short reprieve at my house to clear his head. Didn't know how that would happen though since Merlene's here almost every other day.

"David, what you're asking of Lucille is foolish! You have a home. What on earth are you thinking?" Merlene was clearly concerned.

"Mom, I love you, but you've become overbearing," he replied. "I'm a grown man; I'm sick of you trying to run my life."

"David..." she tried to interject, but he stopped her.

"Now, this thing with you and Sabrina has gone too far. If you don't think she's the right one for me, it's my job to find that out, but I'm not leaving home because of that situation. It's because of everything."

He glanced at me, then shifted his focus back to Merlene.

"I didn't want to do this in front of anyone, but Miss Lucille's like family." He paused for a moment. "What I'd planned to do was to move out completely and get myself an apartment, but decided instead to just take a little break and clear my head."

I was right on.

"Maybe after a while, I'll be back home, but things would have to change or I'm going back to plan A which is to get an apartment and leave for good."

I sensed Merlene was humbled by David's assertion and his poignant, yet subtle threat. I knew her greatest fear in life was losing him – and that would be in any way, shape or form. Moving out for good because she'd chased him off by dominance was worse than him deciding it was time to just venture out on his own. It seemed like a good ten years before she responded. It probably was the very first time I'd noticed my friend at a loss for words.

"Well, David... if that's how you feel. I mean... if being here is what you think you need, I won't try to stop you," she finally uttered, almost in a whisper.

My heart went out to her, but she knew she'd always see the boy because my house was just like her second home. I kind of wondered at first why David chose to come here instead of staying somewhere else for a while. He must have known by making such a move, he wasn't really getting away from his mother. Then it hit me that he was just trying to prove a point to her – to use this step as a warning so that he didn't have to do the thing she dreaded most which was to leave permanently. Smart kid. A kind one too.

"So, can I rent the room, Miss Lucille?" he asked.

I sighed deeply. "Seems fine with your mother; so the answer, my son, is yes. You can have the room for as long as you like."

"Great!"

"Now, bear in mind, there are rules. There'll be no drinking alcohol or smoking in my house; no shacking up in any of these bedrooms with any women – or men for that matter." I got the stare of shock when I said that, but I didn't care. He had to be told the rules just like all the others who'd rented rooms in my house. "The TV room, living room and front porch can be used for privacy when visitors come over. Everyone here can use the kitchen, but must each buy their own food and clean up their own mess. This is not a bed and breakfast, ya hear?

"I hear you, ma'am," he replied with a chuckle.

"That's good. And one other thing… no peeing on the toilet seat. You boys need to learn how to aim straight. As a cautionary method, please raise the seat. There'll be no special treatment because of your mother. You must obey the rules like everyone else." I raised my chin. "So, if the laws I've set down don't sit well with you, it would be best to walk right out of that door with your mother."

"Understood," he said. "When can I move in?"

"Anytime you're ready, sonny."

David went out and grabbed a large luggage bag from the trunk of his car. Merlene and I were surprised he'd wasted no time packing up his things and tagging them along.

I showed him to his room while Merlene waited downstairs. David stayed long enough to unpack his bag and then he was gone. Said he'd return in a couple of hours. We figured he'd gone to spend some time with Juliet.

"Can you believe that kid?" Merlene exclaimed.

I shook my head. "I told you, Merlene. You were gonna drive that boy away. I just never imagined he'd end up in my direction. No need to worry though; I'll keep a good eye on him."

"There you go joking again when we're discussing a serious matter, Lucille! My son just walked out on me and to *you*—my best friend! I'm so ashamed right now, I don't know what to do with myself."

"You can't be serious with that!" I grinned.

"What?"

I knew she was even more annoyed. "You said you're so ashamed!"

"That's right!"

"Well, it's not like he set you straight in front of strangers. Like he said, we're all practically family. You've never one day been ashamed of anything that happened in my presence. You're just making the matter seem far worse than it is."

Merlene was quiet for a few moments, perhaps pondering my assertion. "I guess you're right."

"The boy didn't disrespect you, my friend. He did what he did out of love because he doesn't want your relationship to be destroyed for good. Give the young man his space—which means don't go and *up* your visits here just to be checking on him. When he sees you're being mature about the whole thing, he'll be outta here and back with Momma in no time," I said.

VISIT TANYA-R-TAYLOR.COM TO GET 'BLIND SIGHT' TODAY OR CHECK ONLINE WITH YOUR FAVORITE BOOK RETAILER.

FICTION TITLES BY TANYA R. TAYLOR

Tanya-r-taylor.com

* LUCILLE PFIFFER MYSTERY SERIES
Blind Sight
Blind Escape
Blind Justice
Blind Fury

INFESTATION: A Small Town Nightmare (The Complete Series)

* THE REAL ILLUSIONS SERIES
Real Illusions: The Awakening
Real Illusions II: REBIRTH
Real Illusions III: BONE OF MY BONE
Real Illusions IV: WAR ZONE

* CORNELIUS SAGA SERIES
Cornelius (Book 1 in the Cornelius saga. *Each book in this series can stand-alone.*)
Cornelius' Revenge (Book 2 in the Cornelius saga)
CARA: Some Children Keep Terrible Secrets (Book 3 in the Cornelius saga)
We See No Evil (Book 4 in the Cornelius saga)

The Contract: Murder in The Bahamas (Book 5 in the Cornelius saga)
The Lost Children of Atlantis (Book 6 in the Cornelius saga)
Death of an Angel (Book 7 in the Cornelius saga)
The Groundskeeper (Book 8 in the Cornelius saga)
Cara: The Beginning - Matilda's Story (Book 9 in the Cornelius saga)
The Disappearing House (Book 10 in the Cornelius saga)
Wicked Little Saints (Book 11 in the Cornelius saga)
A Faint Whisper (Book 12 in the Cornelius saga)
'Til Death Do Us Part (Book 13 in the Cornelius saga)

* THE NICK MYERS SERIES
Hidden Sins Revealed (A Crime Thriller - Nick Myers Series Book 1)
One Dead Politician (Nick Myers Series Book 2)

Haunted Cruise: The Shakedown
The Haunting of MERCI HOSPITAL
10 Minutes before Sleeping

Printed in Great Britain
by Amazon